THE TITUSVILLE COUNTRY

For the residents of Titusville the arrival of two dark strangers prompted a bizarre and sinister string of events. There were two killings, the appearance and disappearance of a hated former Confederate general, and finally, the partnership of their town marshal with one of his jailhouse inmates.

For Town Marshal Gil Beeman, things were tough. The town was pretty much out of control, and it takes the help of fellow marshal Doug Hall and a crazed female grizzly bear to get things back on the right tracks again.

The Titusville Country

GEORGE FLYNN

A Black Horse Western

ROBERT HALE · LONDON

© George Flynn 1989
First published in Great Britain 1989

ISBN 0 7090 3614 0

Robert Hale Limited
Clerkenwell House
Clerkenwell Green
London EC1R 0HT

Photoset in North Wales by
Derek Doyle & Associates, Mold, Clwyd.
Printed in Great Britain by
WBC Print Ltd., Barton Manor, Bristol.
Bound by WBC Bookbinders Limited.

One
A Hot Springtime Day

When Chief Moore told a Dewlap rider to jump, the feller not only jumped, he asked how high he should jump. The interesting thing about this was that Moore was not a big, brawling man. He was about forty-five, was no more than average height and with rocks in his pockets did not weigh one hundred and seventy five pounds. He was not particularly impressive except that he was honed down to bone and sinew, had good features, pale blue eyes that looked out of a bronzed face, was grey around the temples, and had been Dewlap's rangeboss, and more, for about twelve years, and the Dewlap cow ranch was one of the largest, if not the largest cow-calf ranch for a lot of miles in any direction.

Dewlap was owned by an association of wealthy investors in the East, between Washington and Boston. Occasionally one of the owners would bring his family 'West' for a vacation, but not so often it interfered with Chief Moore's fulltime occupation, which was to make Dewlap pay.

There was another reason people heeded Chief Moore. All Dewlap supplies were purchased from the merchants of Titusville, which was eight miles east of Dewlap's main yard. With five fulltime riders, the rangeboss and the cook, Dewlap's contribution to the Titusville economy was respectable. Titusville merchants from the town blacksmith to the medical practitioner to the proprietor of the general store, considered Chief Moore a friend, and while that probably arose from a personal, pecuniary interest, Fred Barton, Titusville's silversmith-gunsmith who had done no more than twenty dollars' worth of trade with Dewlap or its foreman in ten years, thought highly of Chief Moore even though he had never more than very marginally profited from their acquaintanceship.

Moore was not a complex individual. He worked his ranch, which included his riders. He culled close to the bone when the time came for making up a drive of cattle that probably would not winter well; when there was little work to be done, he led off on the ride to town, but when there was work to be done, Sunday was just another day.

Fred Barton had once commented to Titusville Town Marshal Gil Beeman that if Chief Moore had been a clock a man would be able to set his watch by him. He was that predictable.

Twelve years on the same job, doing it not just well, but also profitably, earning respect along the

way, being liked by the people who worked for him
and many who did not, never deviating from what
appeared to be a dedication to principles and integ-
rity and rectitude, certainly lent substance to the
gunsmith's comment to the town marshal.

It also, in the mildly acerbic opinion of Dorothy
Freeman, the handsome widow of Jed Freeman
who had driven stages for the Overland Company
for nine years before a mud-slide buried him, his
hitch and coach under about three hundred tons of
mountainside, made for a very dull individual.

But Dorothy Freeman was prudent about confid-
ing this conflicting opinion of a genuine paragon of
the cow country. People who liked Chief Moore
were almost invariably not only very loyal, but
quick to defend him against derogators, even ones
who were not only female, extremely good-looking,
and who now owned the Titusville franchise of the
Overland Stage Company, but who headed-up
some of the more prestigious female organizations
around the area, including the Baptist Lady's
Altar Society, The Titusville Committee for Community Development, which was dedicated to
enticing the telegraph company to bring its 'sing-
ing wires' to town, and the Benevolent Aid Society,
whose purpose was to seek out and look after the
needy, the indigent, the orphaned.

It was this last organisation headed by Dorothy
Freeman, that had the old gaffers living in tar-
paper shacks at the lower end of town very close to
being up in arms. They were anachronisms to a
man. Old buffalo hunters, Indian scouts, jerkline

freighters, horse traders whose vocation quite often had led them into temptation when loose horses were encountered which had not been branded.

Dorothy's ladies would descend upon the old men bringing soap, clean hand-me-down clothing, shaving material and unfailingly, The Word.

They absolutely refused to fetch along a jug, some sweet molasses-cured Kentucky twist chewing tobacco, denounced the use of these things in ringing terms, and after a couple of hours of harassment, would shake the dust from their ankle-length skirts and hike back up toward the 'decent' part of town leaving the old men venomous-eyed, wetly mouthing terrible imprecations, and less hair-raising but very blasphemous denunciations, very upset and completely out of their comfortable daily routines. It did no good to complain to Town Marshal Gil Beeman because, although he sympathised with the old scarecrows, Beeman liked his job; Dorothy had more substance than a lot of the menfolk around town and she could be a Tartar when angered, while the scrawny old mostly unshaven, unwashed and whiskey-scented scarecrows were not only few in numbers, and each passing year getting to be fewer, but they did not sit on the Town Council and never had. Dorothy sat on it. In fact she was chairman this year, which happened to also be the year Gil Beeman's contract came up for renewal.

The old men went scuttling over to Harry

Lipton's saloon, The Silver Palace, which had no silver and had been constructed of peeled logs and had a mud-wattle roof from which grass and weeds grew with extravagant abandon every springtime, to wheedle Harry out of a bottle of dregs, which he sold to them, carefully counted out the coins they put up collectively, then leaned on his bar watching them shuffle swiftly back out into the sunshine heading southward.

A thin, tall rangeman mantled with dust and darkened with sweat had watched Harry's transaction with the old men from a short distance up the bar northward. He also watched the old gaffers go flinging out of the saloon, flapping their arms like birds, and he pushed his empty beer glass aside as he said, 'How come you sell whiskey at two-bits a jolt to other folks, and sell a whole bottle to those old men for fifty cents?'

Harry, who was a large, pale, fleshy man with thin hair and hands the size of small hams, straightened up from watching the roadway doors as he replied. He pointed to the cowboy's empty beer glass. 'There's always maybe ten or twelve spoonsful in the bottom of those glasses. The same with whiskey glasses. I keep an empty jug below the counter – like this, see? – and I empty the glasses into the bottle. Sometimes it'll take five, six days to fill the bottle. Sometimes, if there's a drive passin' along, or lots of folks in town like on a Saturday, I can fill a bottle in only maybe two days.'

The tall cowboy had eyed the bottle Harry had

held up for him to see. He scowled. 'You save the
dregs from the beer an' whiskey, wine and
whatnot and pour it all together in one of them
bottles?'

'Yep.'

'That'd poison a rattlesnake, for Cris'sake.' The
cowboy stared at Harry Lipton, his gaze turning
mildly hostile. 'You're goin' to kill them just so's
you can squeeze an' extra half dollar out of –.'

'Naw,' Harry said in disagreement. 'It's the only
way I know to have what they need when they
want it. An' since I figured out to do it about six,
seven years back, to my knowledge it hasn't killed
any of them.'

The cowboy was still scowling when a dusty
customer walked in out of the heat to beat his coat
and trousers with his hat before approaching the
bar. Harry Lipton had grown long in the tooth in
the saloon business. He could read a man like
some folks read books. This dusty, sun-darkened,
lean stranger with his very dark eyes and curly
dark hair, and his thin, sharp features topped off
with a bloodless slit of a mouth as straight and
tight as a bear trap, was not in Harry's view, a
run-of-the-mill stranger.

Harry set up the bottle and jolt glass and
remained in place across the bar until the
whipcord-built dark-eyed man had filled his glass
to the brim, raised it without spilling one drop,
and sent its contents straight down before
speaking. 'I been needing that for a week,' he said,
ignoring Harry to fill the little glass again. Before

raising it this time, he eyed Harry from an expressionless face. 'Does summer always arrive so early in this country?' he asked.

Harry drew the bar-rag from his belt and methodically dried his hands. He did this out of habit, without even thinking about it. 'No. Usually we get a rainy season. But not lately.'

The stranger dropped his second jolt down and shoved the sticky glass aside, leaned on the bar and said, 'Drought?'

Harry was stuffing the rag back under his belt when he answered. 'No. I don't think so, anyway. Usually we get a period of this hot summer weather for a couple of weeks, then the rains start.' He grinned a trifle wryly. 'I hope they start. If they don't, if this heat continues, it'll be a drought summer. Folks in this part of the country would prefer just about anything but that.'

The stranger nodded, continued to lean but no longer was interested in the bottle or the little glass. He looked past Harry at his reflection in the backbar mirror. He was drawn-looking, tired. He leaned back to light a thin cigar then set his back against the bar and watched roadway traffic stirring dust outside.

When Harry returned from drawing off tepid beer for a pair of Dewlap rangemen, the stranger faced back around and he was sweating. It had to be the whiskey because Harry's big old barn saloon was ten degrees cooler inside than the roadway was outside.

He said, 'They got a hotel in Titusville?'

There was one, actually more nearly a room-inghouse but its proprietor preferred having it called a hotel. 'Across the road and northward. Couple of big old shaggy trees growing out front of the porch. You can't miss it.' Harry accompanied his directions with an arm-gesture. 'It's not a boardinghouse. You can't get fed up there, but it's got plenty of rooms.'

The stranger mopped off sweat. 'I hope you're right about that rain,' he said. 'I come from a cold country. I'm sure not used to so much heat this time of year.'

After the stranger departed Harry put away the bottle, dropped the jolt glass into a tub of greasy cold water beneath the bar, and raised his head as one of the Dewlap riders drily spoke.

'We been guessin' what that gent does for a living. Care to toss in your two bits' worth, Harry?'

It was a while before the saloonman answered. He was aware of a cardinal rule of saloon owners: Be damned awful tactful. 'Hard to say,' he told the riders.

One of them laughed. 'Yeah, sure. Well, Jim figured him to be either a lawman or a gunfighter.'

Harry was drying his hands again when he looked up the bar at them. 'How about you?' he asked.

The stained, clear-eyed cowboy still had his sardonic twinkle in his eye when he replied. 'I don't know. He could be a cattle buyer, a travelling man, maybe he's a horse trader with a string of animals tied to trees somewhere beyond town, but one thing he sure as hell is, Harry.'

'What's that?'

'Dangerous,' the cowboy said while picking out small silver coins to place beside his empty glass.

When the Dewlap riders departed Harry had the saloon to himself. It was too early for business. He pulled out the rag and went over to start drying glasses he'd dropped into the tub below the bar.

When Gil Beeman came in later he'd mention the black-eyed stranger. Any stranger to Titusville was a source of local interest and speculation, although from now on with itinerant riders drifting through looking for work, local interest was a lot less lively that it was during late autumn, winter and early spring.

Harry finished with the little glasses, arrayed them in precise ranks along his backbar, stuffed the rag under his belt and went looking for a cigar he'd put aside earlier when it had gone out.

He located it, lighted it, got up a good head of strong smoke and groped under the bar for a dog-eared newspaper some stage passenger had left behind.

Unless those old scarecrows from the lower end of town came in as they frequently did to take over one of his card tables near the window and began a game of toothpick-poker, Harry would have peace and quiet for maybe a couple of hours.

Two
Something Not So Simple

Dorothy Freeman was about thirty-five. She was tall for a woman, about five feet and six inches. She had wavy chestnut hair and grey eyes. In all the ways that men gauged beauty in a woman, she measured up, but actually Dorothy had too much character in her face to be beautiful. She was handsome. She had a strong jaw, a direct gaze, a broad rather than high forehead and beautiful white teeth when she smiled, which was not very often.

She had been a widow six years, had used the savings she and her husband had squirreled away to buy out the previous franchise owner, and although everyone in town had been certain she would be unable to run a stage line, put up with the raffish, foul-talking men who worked as hostlers at the corralyard, or boldly face up to the myriad responsibilities which went with such an undertaking, she had done it all without a qualm, and that of course set her up for disapproval among menfolk.

But not with the womenfolk of Titusville. Dorothy Freeman became their local epitome of those suffragettes back east who went around smashing up saloons with axes and demanding such wildly radical things as the right to vote.

Dorothy never went that far, but when she was required to have a face-down with a man, she did it, as now, when she declined Marshal Beeman's gallant offer of a chair in his office, and did not observe range-country etiquette by mentioning the weather, the price of beef, the infernal politicians back in Washington, and while remaining on her feet looked Beeman squarely in the eye as she spoke straight out by saying, 'There was an attempt to stop my southbound coach five miles north of town by a lone highwayman. He didn't succeed because aside from the driver there were three armed passengers inside. They ran him off with gunfire.'

Beeman leaned back looking up at her. 'Four men shooting at him? Didn't they hit him?'

'No. He was firing back. He didn't hit anyone but he riddled my stage.'

Gil Beeman got stolidly to his feet. 'An' you want me to up there an' track him down?'

Dorothy did not have to raise her gaze very much to meet his eyes. He was taller than she was but standing as indignantly erect as she now was, she seemed taller. 'I want you to find him, Gil. They're like wolves; you may scare them off but they come back.'

Beeman nodded. 'What did he look like?'

'Dark, the passengers said. A lean man of average height with dark curly hair, black eyes, a lipless mouth. He was dressed in dark clothing. The driver said that whoever he was, he knew enough to approach a coach from the near side and to have picked a place to stop the stage where there was plenty of timber and rocks. When he had to retreat the whip said he ducked out of sight among some trees and boulders in moments. Gil, that man is an experienced highwayman. If you don't get him, sooner or later he'll stop a coach or kill people.'

'Maybe he got scairt enough to leave the country, Dorothy.'

Her gunmetal grey eyes hardened. She did not offer a rebuttal to his statement, she simply said, 'You'd better get him, Gil,' and marched back out of the jailhouse office leaving Beeman standing at his desk looking after her.

Later, when he was getting relief from the unusually hot springtime day at The Silver Palace, that near holdup had taken precedence over every other topic, including the continuing heat and the cloudless sky. He listened to the speculations, most of which were pretty wild, and was ready to depart when Harry Lipton came down the counter and leaned to say, 'There was a feller in here a few days back that fit the description of the highwayman right down to the boots.'

Beeman considered the round, fleshy, sweaty face of his old friend. 'Stranger?' he asked.

'Yep. Never saw him before in my life. He wanted

to know if it was always this hot around the Titusville country this time of year, an' asked where the hotel was.'

'Didn't mention where he was from or his name, did he?'

Harry straightened back beginning to scowl. Another cardinal rule among saloon-owners was: Avoid asking questions, particularly personal ones.

Beeman saw the indignant glare, smiled, paid for his beer and spoke as he was turning away. 'No harm in asking. A man might get lucky.'

Harry remained silent and glaring until Marshal Beeman had departed, then went back up the bar where several customers needed re-fills.

The town marshal went down to the livery barn where his two horses were boarded, saddled one and with an eye on the location of the sun, left town up the back alley heading for the place that aborted robbery had occurred.

After the stage road left the foothills the land was open, almost completely treeless, and except for fields of boulders infrequently scattered over a very wide area far from the road itself, did not fit Dorothy Freeman's description of the area where the attempted robbery occurred.

But several miles farther up-country where the foothills began, where the road started a long-spending rise toward the distant notch where it passed through the mountains, there were stands of timber and fields of rocks. Beeman did not anticipate difficulties nor did he have any. For one thing the arrow-straight tyre ruts made just one wild sashay. From that spot the marshal scouted on foot until he found where a horse had been tied. There, he also found shucked-out six-gun loads where the highwayman had paused to reload after the stagecoach had picked up speed heading for town.

He pocketed them, followed the tracks left by the departing horse for half a mile through rock fields and timber, then turned back, eyed the sun's position once more, and headed for town. Gil Beeman did not like missing meals. He'd missed a lot of them in his lifetime but not lately, and habit had a pretty good hold of a man by the time he was in his mid-thirties.

Sunset was on the way by the time he rode down the same back-alley to the livery barn, handed his reins to the dayman and went back up to the jailhouse.

Maybe Fred Barton could tell something from the casings he had brought back but to Gil Beeman they did not look any different from any other forty-five casings. He returned them to his pocket and headed for the cafe.

The place was fairly full despite the fact that it was a mite early for supper. The moment he sat down the questions came. Beeman smiled a lot and shook his head. In a place like Titusville where there was no telegraph and the only newspapers were months old when they reached town, anything as titillating as a stage robbery, successful or not, would be a source of discussion until the cows came home.

Beeman had learned long ago never to confide in anyone about his manhunts. He did not do it now. After he left the cafe the speculation achieved new heights, only now it was about equally divided between those who insisted Beeman knew something and was keeping it to himself, and those who spoke out in clear disgust, claiming that Marshal Beeman was too accustomed to sitting in the comfort of his office to do anything that might cause him personal inconvenience, like running down a highwayman.

Only the cafeman, a grizzled old rangerider with store-bought teeth that had the embarrassing habit of dropping closed while his mouth was open and he was still talking, took a chance and made what was for him a long statement.

'If that subbitch is in the country Gil'll get him. Mark my word.'

Like most judgements based upon personal feelings, this one was more nearly a hope than a conviction, except that Marshal Beeman went up to talk to the grumpy proprietor of the hotel, and had Dorothy Freeman's description of the dark man confirmed, and also picked up an interesting bit of trivia: The dark man had left early in the morning of the day the attempted holdup occurred and had not returned to the hotel until evening.

Gil went down to the livery barn and thought he had struck gold when the liveryman showed him a stalled horse that belonged to the man whose description Beeman had given him, and verified that the day of the shootout up yonder, the horse had come in looking tucked up and ridden down.

Beeman looked the stranger's outfit over. The saddle bore the imprint of a maker in Miles City, Montana. The saddlebags were gone, but they would have been anyway if their owner intended to lie over in Titusville for a while.

Encouraged by good fortune, Marshal Beeman stopped at the cafe for an early dinner. Harry Lipton was half through a meal at the counter. He looked around when Beeman sat down, nodded and went on eating.

They did not even exchange a grunt until the saloonman had finished by which time Marshal Beeman was half-way through his own meal. Harry politely belched behind his upraised hand, then tapped Beeman on the shoulder, leaned close and said, 'You find that feller?'

Gil went on chewing as he shook his head.

Harry inched still closer so as not to be heard by the few other diners. 'There's another one.'

That made Beeman pause and turn slightly to regard the older man. 'Another what?'

'Stranger who's travel stained, sort of tight-lipped and asked about the hotel.' Harry paused until Marshal Beeman's unwavering stare showed that Harry had the lawman's full attention, then he added a little more. 'Sort of dark feller. He wasn't real friendly. Asked some questions then left.'

Beeman resumed his meal without commenting,

but after Harry had departed he paid the cafeman and returned to the livery barn. This time, though, the liveryman shook his head. He hadn't taken in a horse since that other stranger had arrived in town, hadn't seen any strangers in several days excepting a pair of soldiers on their way south to a new post. They had passed through last evening. He only noticed them when they stopped at the smithy just as the town blacksmith was locking up, and talked him into replacing a shoe one of their animals had cast.

Beeman went the full length of town on the east side, found the roominghouse proprietor out back propping up a dilapidated grape arbour, and had to help tamp ground around a replacement upright before he was told that there had been no new roomers since that dark feller had checked in some days back.

At the jailhouse office Beeman stoked up his stove, set the coffee pot on it, and leaned in the roadside doorway. There was an explanation about the absence of the second dark man; he wouldn't be either the first nor last traveller who preferred camping beyond town to the hotel.

Nevertheless, it was disappointing to discover that his earlier, encouraging success, which he had been so sure would resolve the issue of Dorothy Freeman's highwayman, was now clouded by the arrival in Titusville of another man who, according to Harry Lipton, seemed to be stamped from the same mould.

Of course this second stranger did not have to

be in any way involved with the first dark man.
Probably wasn't.

Harry went back for a cup of coffee and was
filling his cup at the stove when Stan Hamelin the
liveryman came across from the cafe sucking his
teeth and looking thoughtful as he walked in.
When Beeman turned holding his cup of java the
liveryman said, 'You was in earlier askin' about a
dark feller – a stranger?'

Beeman nodded on his way to his desk-chair.

The liveryman sat down still sucking his teeth.
He stopped long enough to say, 'Well, just as I was
headin' up to the cafe for supper a feller rode in on
a big sorrel horse and paid for the animal's keep
with silver dollars.'

'What was his name?'

'He didn't give it an' I didn't ask it. I left him
with my dayman but as I was eatin' I saw him
walking northward in front of the jailhouse with
saddlebags slung over his shoulder.' The
liveryman stopped making his annoying noises.
'Goin' up to the hotel, I expect.'

Beeman had a question: 'Dark feller?'

The liveryman nodded. 'Sort of. Dark hair
anyway, but the rest of it looked to me like it had
come from bein' in the sun an awful lot, an' his
eyes were sort of hazel, not real dark.'

Beeman tasted the coffee, lingered over that
until he'd decided he would see what he could find
out about this third stranger, then pushed the cup
aside and shrugged his shoulders. Strangers came
and went. It was a little early in the year for that

kind of traffic yet, but he'd seen it happen before; rangemen arriving hoping to be the early birds when cowmen started hiring.

He thanked the liveryman, who departed, and decided to go up to the roominghouse. If one stranger had not engaged a room up there, two had. At least one had, the first stranger, and there was a good possibility the latest stranger had.

Before he did anything else, Gil had to meet at least one of those strangers. Preferably the one whose description seemed to fit the highwayman.

He got as far as the roadway door when three horsemen turned in at the jailhouse tie-rack, swung down, looped their reins and nodded at Marshal Beeman.

The first rider to walk into the office was Chief Moore of the Dewlap outfit. The other two men were Dewlap riders. Beeman knew them all, and while he was slightly annoyed at their appearance at this particular moment, he trooped back inside with them.

Chief Moore was pulling off his roping gloves when he said, 'Gil, do you know a feller named Alfred Pierce?'

Beeman shook his head. 'Not that I recollect. What about him?'

'Dark feller,' Moore said, folding the gloves over his shellbelt. 'Black curly hair, black eyes, sort of weasel-faced, maybe thirty, thirty-five years old. Wears dark clothes.'

Beeman leaned on the front of his desk. 'Pierce?'

'Yeah,' replied Chief Moore, digging something

out of a pocket. 'We think that was his name. Anyway, that's the name engraved on the backstrap of this little under-and-over bellygun.'

Beeman accepted the big-bored little nickel plated weapon. It was loaded. It was an efficient gun only at very close range. It could blow a man out of a chair at a poker table but at any greater distance was unreliable. The name on the backstrap of the little gun was Alfred Pierce.

The Dewlap men found places to sit and were watching the town marshal. When he mentioned the name, Chief Moore made a bone-dry comment. 'Deader'n a damned rock.'

Beeman put the bellygun on his desk and scowled. 'Pierce?'

'Yeah. You know Cliffy here. Well, he was combin' the foothills to turn back strays, was up among the trees a ways and come onto this dead man. We went up with a wagon and brought him back to the ranch. He had that gun in a little boot-holster. The rest of his belongings are at the ranch along with the carcass. You can have 'em just by drivin' out with a wagon.' Chief was looking steadily at Marshal Beeman. 'Down at the livery barn Stan Hamelin showed us a horse a man answerin' Pierce's description put up a few days back. Gil; if it's the same man – how in the hell did he bring his horse back here, leave it down yonder, when he was already dead up in the foothills of our range?'

Beeman gave a reasonable answer. 'Wasn't the same man. Couldn't have been.'

'We described him to Stan. He said it fit the feller who brought in his rode-down horse to a fare-thee-well.'

Beeman smiled. 'Chief, it could not have been.' At the look he was getting from the Dewlap boss he added a little more. 'All right. I'll get a wagon and drive out tomorrow, early. And I'll bring Harry Lipton with me. He just might know this man on sight.' As the Dewlap riders arose Marshal Beeman offered coffee but they had ridden about eight miles with something different in mind.

They left Gil standing in his jailhouse doorway. He had forgotten all about his earlier intention to visit the hotel until the Dewlap men disappeared beyond Harry Lipton's spindle doors, then he remembered and went hiking northward with late evening bringing fresh coolness as it spread shadows around the countryside.

Three
A Dead Man

The hotel proprietor listened to everything Beeman had to say wearing his customary expression of scepticism. His answer was to lead the way to a locked door, unlock it without a word and step aside.

He watched the marshal rummaging through a set of saddlebags for a moment before saying, 'Instead of giving me that long-winded description of the feller, why didn't you just say you wanted to see inside the room of Amos Pierson?'

Beeman turned slowly. 'Amos Pierson?'

'Yes. The dark, weasel-faced feller who hired this room.'

For a while the marshal continued examining the effects of the man whose room he was in. Then he tossed the saddlebags aside and went to the door. As he passed into the hallway he said, 'Did he sign his name in your book?'

The hotel man glowered. 'I don't keep no book.

They pay in advance or they don't get a room. Beyond that I don't care what their names are. But the description you gave me fits this feller right down to his boots.'

Marshal Beeman blew out a big, ragged breath, went out to the sagging front veranda and stood in the shade for a long time. Yesterday he'd been so confident. All he'd had to do was find the place where a highwayman had tried to stop one of Dorothy's damned stages, and track him until it looked like he was heading out of the country, and today there were two men answering to the same description, neither one of them seemed to be in town, one of them as sure as hell was dead out at Dewlap, and both of them had the same initials.

He went down to the livery barn to look at that horse the liveryman said had come in looking ridden down. The horse was not there and neither was Stan Hamelin. His dayman said he'd gone up to the general store. About the missing saddle animal the dayman knew nothing.

Neither did the liveryman, when Beeman found him talking to one of those old gaffers from the lower end of town. They were standing out in front of the store when Beeman walked up, let them both see him, then leaned indolently waiting for their conversation to end, which it did very shortly. Beeman let the old man walk away but stopped Hamelin in his tracks with a question.

'Where is that horse you said the dark feller brought back all tucked up the day the stagecoach was stopped up north of town?'

Hamelin's stubbly features went slack. He stared steadily at the town marshal for a moment before speaking. 'He's in his stall down at the barn.'

'No he isn't. Your dayman showed me the empty stall. He didn't seem to know when the horse was taken.'

Hamelin continued to stare. 'He ain't there? Well, when I came along to get ready for business this morning ....'

'Yeah?'

Hamelin fidgeted. 'My dayman was already there so I let him do the feedin' an' whatnot. I went up to the cafe, then came over here to the store.'

'In other words you didn't see the empty stall; you didn't know the horse was gone.'

'I guess not.'

'How about the horse of that other stranger, the one you told me about over at my office?'

'His horse was still in the front stall this morning. I saw him as I was walkin' out.'

Hamelin was worried. He could not remember the last time a horse had disappeared from his barn. He was convinced of one thing; that horse had been in his stall yesterday afternoon, which probably meant it had been removed during the night. Maybe stolen. He looked anxiously at Marshal Beeman. 'Marshal, the feller who owned that horse was a mean-lookin' individual. I think I'd better be sick abed for a few days. If someone stole his animal out of my barn he's not goin' to like it one little bit.'

Beeman straightened up looking northward in

the direction of the saloon. 'Don't get sick just yet,' he said. 'Wait until tomorrow after I get back from a wagon ride.' He looked back at the liveryman. 'I need a team and that light dray wagon you got with the green sides.' Beeman smiled. 'I'll be around for it about sunup tomorrow.'

He left the paunchy liveryman gazing after him and strode up to Lipton's Silver Palace Saloon.

Trade had been brisking up for Harry for the past hour or so; nevertheless, because this was a week-day evening, he did not expect to do any better than he usually did on week-nights. Harry really only made good money on Saturdays.

He welcomed Marshal Beeman with a smile and a wide sweep of his bartop with a sour bar-rag. 'Straight?' he asked. Gil nodded, waited until Harry had returned and said, 'I need you to ride out to Dewlap with me in the morning. We'll leave town before sunup and with any luck be back before supper.'

Lipton watched the lawman fill his little glass without saying a word. When the marshal shoved the bottle aside and nodded as he raised the glass, Harry said, 'What for? I got a business to run. I can't be ridin' over the countryside ...'

Beeman held the poised small glass inches from his lips when he interrupted Lipton. 'You don't even unlock the front door until ten o'clock, Harry, an' aside from the old men from the south end of town, you don't do any business until late afternoon.'

Beeman downed the whiskey, pushed the glass aside and leaned, smiling at the fleshy, large barman as Lipton asked a question.

'What for? What's out at Dewlap?'

'A dead man who fits your description of a man whose name was most likely Alfred Pierce.'

Lipton's cheeks puffed up then emptied. 'That dark feller?'

'Yes.'

'Dead?'

'Yes.' Beeman straightened up off the bar, turned and walked out of the saloon. Lipton stared at his back until he was out of sight, then looked down. The bottle was there, as was the little jolt glass, but no money.

He swore, swept up the bottle and glass, stalked up as far as his tub of greasy wash-water behind the bar, dropped the glass in and put the bottle back on the shelf. As he was turning he spoke to himself. 'Before sunup! I don't even get to bed until past midnight. That's why I don't open for business until ten in the morning. Sunup, for Chris'sake!'

It also occurred to him that there had to be other people around town who could identify that dark stranger; Stan Hamelin, for example, or the old gnome who ran the hotel.

Nevertheless, despite his reluctance, he was stamping around down at the livery barn watching the nightman who was putting an unmatched pair of horses on a light wagon with green sides when Marshal Beeman arrived looking fresh, shaved and cheerful. Harry'd had one fast cup of hot coffee otherwise he probably wouldn't even have nodded as the nighthawk led the hitch out front and handed Beeman the lines. He too, was not in a talkative mood. After the pair of townsmen were driving up out of town the nightman spat aside, went back to the warmth of the harness room and sank down in semi-darkness atop a pile of stiff and smelly blankets to catch another forty winks before the day's business began.

It was cold, the air was still and there were paling stars glittering like creek-pebbles all across a cloudless sky. Gil shook his head. 'I thought sure it was goin' to rain last week.'

Lipton remained stolidly wrapped inside his coat, neck pulled down inside the turned-up collar of his coat, looking stonily straight ahead. He did not speak until they were mid-way along and the sun was brightening the vastness of their area. Then all he said was: 'Where'd you get the name Alfred Pierce?'

'Off the backstrap of a bellygun Chief Moore handed me yesterday when he rode to town to tell me one of his riders had found a dead man on their foothill range. A *dark* dead man.'

Harry thought about that for another half mile. 'It don't have to be the same man. Lots of fellers around with that dark look.'

Gil agreed. 'Sure are. Night before last someone took a horse out of Hamelin's barn. Neither Stan nor his hostler knew anything about it.'

Lipton's curiosity prompted him to raise his head slightly and turn his gaze at the lawman. 'The dark feller's horse?'

'Well, that's where the trouble starts, Harry. Y'see, the dark feller brought his horse back to Stan's barn the night of that attempted holdup of Dorothy's stage.'

'What's wrong with that?'

'If the feller out yonder I need you to identify for me was dead in the foothills after he tried to stop the stage, how the hell did he ride his horse back to town?'

Lipton's head went down into the turned-up collar of his coat. It was still chilly, even with the sun climbing. It remained that way all the way to Dewlap's yard where the riders were rigging out for the day's work. By the time Beeman and Lipton reached the yard only Chief Moore, who had known the marshal was coming and for that reason had remained behind, the ranch cook and the chore-boy were also in the yard, the other men had ridden westward to scatter out looking for sore-footed bulls.

It was just one of the annoyances of the cow-calf business that because bulls had to walk a lot further than cows looking for scent, they got tender-footed. When that happened they forgot about breeding cows, sought muddy places, and stayed there. The usual result was fewer calves the following spring.

Beeman saw Chief Moore waiting for them in front of the log barn. As they rattled past the cookshack the *cocinero* waddled out to the porch drying his hands on a grey towel and called out that there was hot coffee inside. Gil waved and kept on driving. He stopped where Moore was waiting. They exchanged greetings as Beeman tied the team then followed the rangeboss down into the gloomy large old barn. Harry trooped along, no longer with his head tucked in like a turtle, but still wearing the coat.

Moore opened a stall door and moved back. Beeman stepped over straw bedding and knelt to lift the blanket covering the dead man. He turned.

'Harry?'

Lipton walked in, leaned, looked for a long time then straightened back. 'That's him,' he said and walked out of the stall.

Chief Moore leaned on the door watching Marshal Beeman examine the corpse. 'Shot,' he laconically said. 'In the back.'

Beeman had to push aside some clothing to find the holes. There had been bleeding, but not very much, and as the saloonman was finally unbuttoning his coat he said, 'Pretty small hole where the slug came out, Gil. Steel-jacketed bullet you reckon?'

Beeman was leaning over concentrating on his work and did not reply, but when he finally arose to leave the stall he said, 'Harry, that bullet was pretty high.'

Lipton nodded. 'Killed him quick, eh?'

The marshal stood gazing at his old friend. 'Yeah, quick. Then how in the hell did he ride his horse back to town and leave it at the livery barn?'

Chief Moore, who had been watching and listening, made another laconic remark. 'If his horse got back to town, sure as hell this gent didn't take it there.'

They walked out front where Lipton flung his coat into the wagon-bed. Moore suggested coffee at the cookshack but Beeman declined. He wanted to get the corpse back to town as soon as possible because this was obviously going to be another hot day, and people who had died violently seemed to swell up faster than folks who died in bed. There was no cover over the wagon-bed and the drive was eight miles.

Four
Murder?

Titusville's medical practitioner was an elderly soul who had the build and quickness of a scrawny old bird. When Marshal Beeman and the saloonman unloaded their corpse at his back shed, the doctor made little sniffing sounds as he walked around the table where they had placed the body.When Beeman said, 'I'd like to know all you can tell me about the slug that killed him, and how it did it,' the old man raised bird-like little shrewd eyes as he replied.

'Got to work fast, Marshal. I can tell you right now, but to earn my two dollars for the autopsy I'll have it for you in the morning. Then you got to get him out of here into the ground. This man didn't die only yesterday y'know.'

Beeman took the liveryman's outfit down the alley to its owner's place of business while Harry Lipton went over to unlock the saloon's doors and light several lamps.

It had not been a particularly trying day, but it had been a long one. Marshal Beeman was relaxing at his desk staring at the ceiling when Dorothy Freeman walked in. Beeman did not arise but he did make one gallant gesture, he removed his hat and let it drop to the floor before offering the handsome woman a chair.

As was her custom, she dispensed with the customary preamble to every range-country conversation, which was considered rude, and said, 'One of my yardmen heard over at Lipton's saloon that you brought back a dead man from Dewlap. He also heard that it was the same man who tried to rob my coach a while back.'

Beeman regarded the handsome woman for a long time in silence. When he finally spoke it was with controlled irritation. 'We brought back a dead man Chief Moore had in his barn. Found dead up in the foothills.'

Dorothy leaned back in her chair. 'The foothills … That's where the highwayman disappeared after the gunfight. At least one bullet did hit him after all, didn't it?'

Beeman continued to regard the woman a little pensively. 'I don't know,' he said quietly. 'I don't know how he got shot or whether it's the same man. It could be. It could also be that his name was Alfred Pierce.'

Dorothy Freeman's gaze hardened. It may have been as much the marshal's seemingly calm, almost indifferent attitude as it could have been his unsatisfactory answers, but whatever it was it angered her. She stood up. 'He tried to rob the stage. He is dead, obviously shot during the attempt, and now you bury him.'

Beeman's gaze did not leave her face even while she was leaving the chair. 'Sure. But I'd like you to explain something to me.'

'What?'

'He rode his horse back to Hamelin's barn the day of the attempted holdup. Got back in the evening.'

She stood staring at the marshal, then sat down again. 'Then it couldn't have been the same man, could it?'

Beeman gently wagged his head. 'Not unless a person believes in horse-riding ghosts, it couldn't have.'

'Gil, there must be two of them.'

He nodded about that too because he had been considering this obvious possibility shortly before she had walked in. 'It's likely. Someone stole that same horse night before last. Snuck him out of the livery barn.'

She sank back in the chair. 'I don't understand,' she murmured, and he smiled for the first time since she'd arrived in his office. 'Does my heart good to hear you admit that, Dorothy. For a while now I been thinkin' maybe you're always right an' I'm always wrong.'

She eyed him warily, seemed about to speak for a moment, but arose and walked out of the office without saying another word.

Marshal Beeman felt better than he'd felt all

day, retrieved his hat and went up to the hotel looking for that third stranger, the one who was not as dark as the other two. He had no reason to believe the stranger was up there, and he was right. The proprietor shook his head even before Beeman had finished giving his description. He said, 'Nope. No one like that. In fact except for that feller whose room you searched and another dark feller, I haven't had a customer in two weeks.'

Beeman walked the full length of town southward and arrived just as Hamelin was departing for the night, leaving everything in the hands of his nighthawk. They met out front and when Beeman asked about the stranger Stan told him about earlier, the liveryman ignored the question to ask one of his own.

'Is that feller you'n Harry fetched back to town from out at Dewlap the same feller whose horse got stoled out of my barn?'

Beeman nodded. 'Seems like it is.'

The liveryman expelled a shaky big breath. 'Thank gawd. I been worried peeless he'd show up an' I'd have tell him his horse been stole.'

'That's why I told you not to go to bed until I got back to town today, Stan,' the lawman explained. 'That may give you cause to stop worrying, but it does just the opposite for me. There's a horsethief somewhere around. I got to find him an' maybe he's more'n just a horsethief. Now then — about that stranger you told me about a couple days back. The not-so-dark-feller. Where is his horse?'

Hamelin turned back into the runway, angled

to his left and halted near one of the front stalls. A large, rawboned sorrel horse stood solemnly looking out at them. Beeman looked for a brand and found none. As he was latching the door closed after himself he said, 'Has his owner been around lately?'

He hadn't. 'Nope. Not since he left the horse here. Well … the way things been goin' lately, maybe I'd just ought to say he ain't been around that I know of. After dark I don't know.'

Beeman walked away. One of those remaining strangers had to be in town tonight, and despite his tiredness he made the rounds looking for him.

What he encountered was not the not-so-dark-man who owned the sorrel horse.

He was mingling with the crowd in Harry's place where tobacco smoke hung overhead in fragrant layers and talkative townsmen, with a sprinkling of freighters, travellers and rangemen, about half-filled the big old lighted room, when Fred Barton edged up and said, 'Harry told me about the dead man.'

Beeman gazed at the gunsmith trying to remember what it was he'd wanted to see him about, then abruptly remembered and dug around for those bullet casings from up where the unsuccessful highwayman had reloaded. He handed them to Fred. 'I'll be around in the morning to hear what you can tell me about those things, and maybe the gun they came from.'

Barton was pocketing the casings when he looked past, then said, 'Harry's makin' faces. I think he wants to talk to you.'

The bar was crowded but evidently if it hadn't been Harry would still have motioned for Beeman to go to the far lower end of the bar. Down there Lipton took Beeman by the arm to a more private place and said, 'Remember I told you another one of those dark fellers came in? Well, he was in here not fifteen minutes ago.'

The marshal stared. 'You're sure it was him?'

'As sure as I am that I'm standin' here right now. He ordered a drink and nursed it for five minutes, then downed it and walked out.'

'Did he say anything.'

'Yeah, that he wanted a drink. That was all. He looked like maybe he'd been riding; sort of dusty and tired.' Harry tapped Beeman on the chest very lightly. 'My guess is that he'll be up at the roominghouse. I can get my shotgun and go up there with you.'

'An' who'd mind the bar? Naw, you stay here.'

'Gil …?'

'Yeah, I know. "Be careful". See you in the morning.'

He barely made it past the spindle doors into the feeble moonlight when a thick, sagging figure came towards him looking worried. It was the liveryman. He stopped, stared a moment, then said, 'That damned horse is back.'

Beeman considered Hamelin's worried expression. 'The one that disappeared out of your barn the other night?'

'The same damned horse, Marshal. I forget

names real easy and sometimes faces, but I never forget a quality, good-lookin' horse.'

Beeman said, 'No wonder you never got married.'

Hamelin's scowl began up around his eyes and travelled down to his lips. If he intended to say something sharp he did not get the opportunity. Beeman had another question for him. 'Who brought him in?'

'I don't know. I been workin' on my books since after supper. When my nightman came along an' went down to the stalls to fork feed, that damned horse was in the same stall, down near the back alley, where he'd been before. I didn't hear anything. If whoever put him in the stall was bein' quiet I wouldn't have heard anything, not that far from the harness room. My nightman came lopin' up lookin' like he'd seen a ghost. I went down there with him and sure as hell – there he was, the same horse.'

'Did he look as tucked up as he had the last time you saw him?'

'No. Not that bad. But he'd been ridden. The saddle sweat was still plasterin' his hair down.'

'Was there a saddle, bridle, blanket?'

'Just the horse. Whoever rode him in took his outfit with him. Leastways we couldn't find it an' we looked all over hell.'

Beeman turned to look up and down the roadway. There were a few animals at some of the tie-racks, not many though, and there was no traffic, not even any pedestrians out to enjoy the balmy night. He looked back to the liveryman. 'Go on in and have a nightcap, but don't mention anything about that horse. Not even to Harry.'

Hamelin nodded. 'Marshal, what in the hell is goin' on?'

Beeman said, 'I wish I knew. Put that horse in a stall up near your harness room, an' if anyone comes after him let me know right away.'

He left the agitated liveryman staring after him as he crossed the dark roadway before turning north in the direction of the roominghouse. But Hamelin did not watch him very long. He needed something to calm his nerves. Appearing and disappearing horses were something he had not encountered before in his many years as a liveryman.

Beeman was mid-way along and was passing the neat cottage of the local medical practitioner when a nearly-falsetto voice hailed him from the dark porch up there. The call sounded a little like the piping of a bird.

He squinted past the picket fence, was called at again, and walked on up to the porch where the doctor was sitting in a rocker smoking a cigar that gave off an aroma which put Marshal Beeman in mind of two aromas combined into one, a tanyard and a clay-floored horse stall.

The doctor removed his cigar, spat into a geranium bed and said, 'You don't have to wait until morning. I finished on that feller. Here, sit down.'

Beeman obeyed. The doctor's porch was a

serene place. There were fragrances reaching it from flowerbeds other than the one filled with geraniums. Beeman removed his hat, settled back and sighed.

The bird-like old man said, 'Nice night but we sure could use some rain.'

Beeman nodded while gazing out into the roadway.

The doctor took another pull off his cigar and held it out to examine the length of ash, which, it was said, was how one could tell if a cigar was good quality or not. 'That feller was killed by a steel-jacketed carbine bullet. Fred Barton can tell more about those things than I can, but I'd guess it was maybe a twenty-five-thirty-five. Small, clean hole.'

'How long did it take to kill him?' Beeman asked.

'Not very long. It ruptured two arteries. He bled internally like a gut-shot bear, but I'd guess he died within ten, at the most fifteen minutes. Mostly the bleedin' was inside. There wasn't much around the bullet holes.' Again the doctor paused to examine the cigar ash. It was longer and it was holding together, but it was also beginning to have an ominous droop. 'Harry gets these things for me from a freighter who brings them over from Albuquerque. Or is it Taos? They're cured in rum. Care to try one, Marshal?'

'No thanks.'

'Don't use 'em eh? But it's got a nice aroma don't you think?'

Beeman turned his head and put a long, steady gaze upon the older man. 'Yeah. Wonderful aroma. If he died within about fifteen minutes of bein' shot, he couldn't have gone very far, could he?'

'No. Maybe no more'n about where he staggered after being hit, Why?'

'Well, I went up there and found where someone had emptied a gun and left the casings where they fell. There'd been a horse tied at the same place.'

'How far from where the attempt was made to stop the stage?'

'Quarter of a mile. Maybe a little more.'

The doctor made one of his sniffing snorts. 'Marshal, that man couldn't have gone a quarter of a mile after he was shot if he'd had wings.' The doctor removed his cigar again but ignored the ash this time as he twisted to frown at Marshal Beeman. 'I think we got to be talking about two men.'

Gil Beeman returned his thoughtful gaze to the distant dark roadway as he replied. 'Yeah. I've been wondering if that wasn't the case for a couple of days now.' He arose, put on his hat and faced the seated older man. 'I'll see if I can round up some fellers to take the body off your hands tomorrow.'

The doctor was puffing again and spoke around the cigar. 'I'd appreciate that. As soon as he's out of my shed I'll take the bill for the autopsy down to Dorothy an' she can get it approved for payment the next time the Town Council sits. By the way, Marshal. That feller was shot in the back. That's murder isn't it?'

There wasn't much of a moon and starlight by itself did not do a whole lot to mitigate the darkness as Beeman again struck out for the roominghouse.

It was not actually late but Titusville was already beginning to turn out its lamps. The Silver Palace was the only bright lighted business establishment the full length of Main Street, but there were a few night-lights glowing here and there. In front of the distant livery barn, for example, where a pair of brass carriage lamps had been mounted on either side of the doorless runway opening, and in the same location, on either side of the log gates at the roadway entrance to Dorothy Freeman's corralyard.

Beyond town the range country, which ran for hundreds of miles, showed no lights at all. Even if there had been ranch buildings close enough to town for their lights to be seen, there still would not have been any. People who did physical work from sunup to sundown did not ordinarily spend very much time marvelling at the mysteries of balmy nights after supper.

By the time Marshal Beeman reached the sagging old porch of the hotel the place was as dark as the inside of a boot. The front door, which was never locked, opened to an aroma of greasy cooking mingled with an assortment of other odours, horsesweat, tobacco, smoking wicks of coal oil lamps and stale air.

He had to roust out the proprietor to get the location of the rooms of the men he wanted to see, and that was an unpleasant interlude. The old man was not pleasant even at his best. When he was shaken awake he glared at Marshal Beeman with bared teeth, but gave the information Beeman wanted without swearing or even snarling. Gil Beeman was over six feet tall and weighed above two hundred pounds. In broad daylight he was impressive, but in gloomy semi-darkness with an eight-foot-tall shadow behind him on the wall, he seemed much taller, much heavier, and unlikely to be shaking someone awake this late at night unless he was dead serious.

After the older man told Beeman which rooms had been paid for by his two latest residents, he raised up slightly in his bed and said, 'That second feller just hired in today. He's taller'n lighter-lookin' than the other feller. I think he might be in his room, but the other one, the darker feller, he comes an' goes, sort of mysterious like. I seen him come in, didn't see him go out, so he ought to be in his room, only I wouldn't bet on it … See that brass key hanging from the nail? Take it with you. It'll unlock any door in the hotel. Take it. I don't want no doors kicked open.'

Five

A Night Beeman Would
Never Forget

In varying degrees two-legged creatures which are endowed – or cursed – with the ability to reason, seem unable to avoid daily disappointments as well as daily interludes of satisfaction.

They are not uncommonly likely to experience these two attributes within a short period of one another. When Gil Beeman very quietly opened the locked door of the man he particularly wanted to interrogate, the surviving dark man, the rear window was open, cooling nighttime air filled the room indicating the window had probably been open for some time, and the room was empty.

He could have searched the absent resident's effects and the idea occurred to him while he was standing in pale darkness looking around, but the disappointment at not finding the man in his room made him anxious to search the other room.

He did not need another disappointment. Nor did he have one, although as he returned to the hallway and re-locked the door, his feeling was that he would have one.

While inserting the pass-key into the second door-lock he exercised the identical caution he'd used at the first door. His reason for stealth had less to do with worrying about awakening someone than it had with getting shot.

The door swung silently inward, there was no gunshot, and because his eyes were now accustomed to the feeble light, he was able to discern a lumpiness to the bed which embodied the precise shape of a sleeping man.

He moved soundlessly inside, paused, then took three long steps to the side of a chair at bedside, leaned to lift out the holstered Colt, and stood a long moment listening to deep sweeps of even breathing. The man's back was to him. During the period of waiting Beeman listened for other sounds. There were a few; an animal was gnawing wood in one of the walls and distantly a dog was raising Cain near the middle or lower end of town, but in the room itself, as well as in the hallway beyond and elsewhere in the roominghouse, there were no menacing sounds.

Gil took one step closer, leaned with the sleeping man's sixgun in his hand and pressed its icy muzzle into the back of the man's neck. There was no movement. Nothing happened except for a slight hitch in the man's breathing, so he pressed a little harder. This time, the hitch was more pronounced and as the normal deep inhalations were resumed they were definitely more shallow.

Gil leaned back and spoke very softly. 'Roll over, put both hands atop the blanket and don't make a sound.'

The man turned very carefully onto his back, put both arms outside the blankets and looked straight up at Marshal Beeman. He was alert; his gaze showed none of the drugged confusion most people showed when they had just been awakened by something unexpected. He looked up, remained absolutely motionless, and after he had accepted the situation his eyes whipped sideways to the chair where his shellbelt and holster were draped, then back to the gun in Gil's hand. He said, 'All right, Marshal. You don't have to cock it ... Chilly night, isn't it?'

Gil did not respond. He kicked the chair around, sat down and methodically plugged out every cartridge in the man's Colt, dropped it back into its holster and leaned forward a little as he said, 'What's your name?'

'Douglas Hall.'

Beeman considered the man's features, which were strong, even and right at this moment, beginning to relax. The man said, 'We were going to meet, but I've been too busy up to now to do anything about that.' The man smiled thinly. 'And the way I figured it, when it happened it might be right here in the hotel.'

Beeman leaned back in the chair. 'Why not just walk into my office down at the jailhouse?'

Douglas Hall hung fire over his reply, then he said, 'Mind if I sit up?'

'Keep your hands outside the blankets.'

As Hall pushed up into a sitting position he ran one set of bent fingers through his tousled hair and wagged his head. 'You ever get the feeling nothing is going right, Marshal?'

Gil almost smiled. 'Yeah. Lately I've felt a lot like that. Who are you, Mister Hall?'

'There's a shirt draped over the back of the chair you're sitting on. Reach into the right-hand pocket.'

Beeman did not move for a while, then he arose, spun the chair so that he had the stranger in sight all the time he was feeling for the shirt pocket, and the moment his fingers encountered cold metal, he stopped watching the bed until he could hold his palm to the weak window-light and see the steel circlet with the star inside it. The embedded black lettering was clearly readable: United States Marshal.

Gil looked toward the bed. Douglas Hall was watching him. When Beeman kicked the chair back around and sat down again he said, 'One time years ago I cornered a horsethief who had one of these things in his pocket.'

Hall looked straight at Beeman when he replied to that. 'Yeah.' His voice was as dry as old corn husks. 'I know that's happened.' He paused a moment then also said, 'I'll tell you something, Marshal. Like the horsethief you caught with one of our badges, any time a man in my line of work rides into a strange community, he's walking on eggs. With your horsethief – stealing horses was his trade – with other kinds of people who break laws it's not that easy to identify them. They don't have someone else's horses with them when they're run down. They have ideas in their minds where you can't see them.'

Beeman settled comfortably in the chair. 'Suppose we just talk sense,' he said, still holding the little badge. 'Let's start with a dark man shot in the back up in the foothills. He's in the local doctor's embalming shed right now. What do you know about him?'

Douglas Hall did not even hesitate. 'His name was Alfred Pierce.'

Gil nodded. 'That's a pretty good opener. Keep talking.'

'He was a hired killer. I don't know a hell of a lot about him but I do know his stamping grounds were over around Council Bluffs.' Hall paused, glanced toward the window, then faced Beeman again. 'I don't want to go into this any further, Marshal.'

Beeman's response was curt. 'Get out of there. Put on your pants. We're goin' down to the jailhouse.' He arose and stepped away from the chair. Douglas Hall arose and got dressed without looking up or speaking until he was reaching for his hat, then he said, 'Like I told you, Marshal. In a strange town men in my line of work don't live long if they're not gawd-awful careful. Do you know what the Knights of the Golden Circle are?'

Gil thought he had heard the name but was uncertain so he shook his head. 'Had something to do with the Civil War didn't they?'

Douglas Hall smiled coldly. 'You are either a hell of an actor, or something else.'

Beeman's eyes widened. 'Actor? Me? Why should I be acting?'

But Douglas Hall was dressed and ready to go. He had even buckled his shellbelt and holstered Colt around his waist. As they left the room he smiled at Gil Beeman but did not say another word until they were down at the jailhouse office. Then, as Beeman worked at building a fire with shavings and kindling, the hazel-eyed man sat down, leaned his chair back and said, 'It almost always happens like this, Marshal. In a strange community I have to take a chance. Sooner or later. You know what I'm talking about?'

Beeman slammed the little iron door as flames licked around the kindling. 'Nope, I sure don't. But if we got to sit in here until the cows come home, you're goin' to tell me.' He went to his desk, sat down and hid a yawn behind the broad back of an upraised hand. 'I'd like you to just tell me straight out what in the hell you are doing in Titusville, how you knew the name of Alfred Pierce, and what all these damned riddles mean.'

Hall seemed willing enough to comply, but as he stared at Gil Beeman he asked a question. 'You know who the President is?'

The town marshal's brows dropped a notch. 'Yeah. I know who the President is. So does everybody else. What's that got to do with anything?'

Hall had another question. 'Do you know who the Secretary of War is?'

This time Marshal Beeman's gaze remained fixed upon the other man. He said nothing but his expression showed a diminishing tolerance.

Hall answered his own question. 'The Secretary of War is Elihu Root. Marshal Beeman, did you ever hear of a Confederate general named Joe Wheeler?'

Beeman leaned on the desktop with both elbows as he said, 'Who is the other dark feller with the room at the top of the hotel?'

Douglas Hall sighed, gazed briefly at the racked up guns along the far wall, and ignored Beeman's questions as he started speaking again.

'General Joe Wheeler is the only former Confederate officer of high rank who volunteered to join the Union army after the war.'

Beeman made a wry comment. 'That must have made him real popular in the South.'

For the first time Douglas Hall smiled. 'You hit the nail on the head. He was denounced throughout the defeated South. In fact he wasn't very popular with a lot of the Northerners who had fought against the Confederacy during the war.' Hall paused to shift position in the chair. 'General Joe Wheeler was on that stagecoach that Alfred Pierce was supposed to stop. He had two staff officers with him. They were on their way down to the border. Pierce's objective was to assassinate

General Wheeler.'

Beeman eased back off his desk very slowly. 'It wasn't an attempted holdup?'

'It was an attempted assassination by a man the Knights of the Golden Circle, a society of Southern Confederacy die-hards, hired to kill the most hated U.S. general officer. Joe Wheeler.'

As he finished speaking Douglas Hall went to stand with his back to the stove. The night was well advanced. It was colder outside than it was inside, but there was a slight chill inside too.

He gazed at Marshal Beeman. 'Now – what I mentioned before – about riding into a town where a man doesn't know a soul, comes up. Thousands of former Confederates went west after the ruin of their nation.' Hall smiled again, thinly, even a little warily. 'There are pockets of the secret order throughout the West. Marshal; even as far off as Oregon Territory, they are very strong. Maybe in Titusville too.' Hall returned to his chair, still faintly, ironically smiling at Gil Beeman. 'I'm unarmed. You caught me sleeping. It's up to you.'

Beeman's brows slowly lowered as he and the other man looked steadily at each other. 'You think I might be one of those Knights of the Golden Circle?'

Hall shrugged. 'You wouldn't be the first lawman, judge or even federal officer who turned out to be one.'

Gil went to the stove, placed his coffee pot atop of it and turned. 'Let me tell you something. I didn't know who the Secretary of War was. I never heard of General Joe Wheeler, and while I think I've heard something about the Knights of the Golden Circle, I'll bet my life there aren't any in the Titusville country. Mister Hall – Marshal Hall if you really are a federal lawman – I don't care a damn about any of your story except the part you haven't made very clear yet; the part about Alfred Pierce, another feller who looks a little like him, and you.'

Hall nodded. 'We could settle some of it if there was a telegraph office in Titusville. You could tele-graph to the U.S. Marshal's office in Washington about me. Since there is no telegraph office ...' Hall smiled again. 'You're going to have to take me at my word. Right now the other man you're interested in, Amos Pierson, is still out there.'

'Why?'

'Because when General Wheeler finishes his business down south he's coming back up through here on his way to Denver where he'll take one of the steam trains back to Washington.'

Gil filled two cups, gave one to the other tall man and returned to his desk with the other cup. As he was sitting down he said, 'Send word to General Wheeler not to come back up the same way.'

Hall was agreeable. 'Sure. Tell me how. There is no telegraph in your town and my guess is that the general and his two staff officers are probably already finished down yonder and are on their way back.'

Gil placed both hands around the coffee cup, felt the warmth and sat gazing into the cup for a long time before speaking again. 'Who shot Alfred Pierce in the back?'

Hall's stare did not waver. 'I did. I was trying to catch them both. They were brothers. I think Pierce was their real name. They hired out to do killings as a team. I tried to overtake them before they got this far west. When they went up your roadway to ambush General Wheeler's stage, I had to skirt back and around through those hills. I didn't get lost but I sure wasted a lot of time keeping out of sight and hearing distance from them.

'I almost made it. I left my horse, took my Winchester and was sneaking down towards the road when Amos Pierson suddenly saw me moving among the trees. I think at first he thought it was his brother because he called out and said, "Get down there, damn it, the stage is coming." When I stopped and raised my saddle-gun he rolled off his rock and ran like hell.

'I could hear the coach coming and moved closer to the road as fast as I could. I didn't see Alfred. He was already down there hiding in some rocks. The stage came through. Alfred ran out to stop it expecting his brother to be back up yonder on his rock to shoot anyone who made a bad move. You can guess the rest. The driver wouldn't stop. Alfred started firing and the men inside the coach fired back. It sounded like a damned war.

'As the stagecoach went ahead with the horses in a belly-down run, I slipped and slithered to catch Alfred Pierce. He turned back in the rocks where he'd ducked down when the passengers fired at him. He was rising up when I saw him. He was looking all around. For his brother I suppose. I yelled at him to throw down his guns. I thought they would be empty but they weren't. He fired at me twice before I could dive behind a tree, then he went scrambling away from the rocks, twisting to fire as he got clear. I got just one clean shot. He went down.'

Gil Beeman had one question. 'How far was he from the rocks when he fell?'

'About three or four yards.'

'Marshal, if his brother didn't fire at you but got back where they had their animals tied, tell me how come I found six empty casings back there? If he fell where you shot him he sure as hell didn't re-load a quarter of a mile away.'

'I re-loaded back there,' Hall said. 'I wanted to catch his brother but when I got up there only one horse was still tied. That's where I re-loaded.'

Gil sat a long time in thought, then arose, took down his keyring and jerked his head for Hall to follow him. If Gil hadn't been so tired, he probably would have been surprised by the federal officer's agreeable disposition. After locking Hall into a cell Beeman said, 'I'm dead on my feet. In the morning we can go over all this again. I just de-loused the bunk last month. I'll fetch you some breakfast in the morning. Good night.'

Douglas Hall held the steel straps of his cell in both hands as he watched Marshal Beeman walk back up the dingy little corridor. Just before the oak door was closed between them, Hall said, 'Good night.'

Beeman tossed down the keyring, closed his stove damper, considered the coffee remaining in his cup, turned his back on it and locked the jailhouse from the outside. He was too tired to even speculate whether or not the other dark man had returned and climbed back through his bedroom window up at the roominghouse.

Six

'Shut Up!'

Beeman slept like a dead man, just not as long. When he awakened the sun was high, Titusville was noisily bustling and someone was warping steel over an anvil.

By the time Beeman shaved, scrubbed, and was ready to eat the rear-end out of a skunk if someone would hold its head, there was rising heat in the day and still not a cloud in any direction.

He ate alone. The cafeman was still cleaning up after the morning trade and had nothing to say. By the time Gil got a little beer-bucket half full of black coffee and another little bucket of beef stew for his prisoner, the mail stage which swept through about mid-morning every day, went rattling past the jailhouse.

Gil's prisoner looked rough and waved away the lawman's offer to take him out back where he could wash and shave. He was hungry, the other things could wait.

As he was watching his prisoner eat, someone wearing spurs walked into the office from the roadway. Beeman turned in that direction.

The visitor was Chief Moore. This time his news was less startling. 'We found a lame horse with our loose-stock yesterday. It might be a bowed tendon but I'm more inclined to believe it's a jammed shoulder. Anyway, he's wearin' a brand I never saw before, an' he's someone's saddle animal.'

'You bring him to town?' Beeman asked.

'No. He's tender as hell and favouring. I wouldn't walk a horse eight miles in his condition. You can come out and look at him, or wait a few weeks an' when's he's able, I'll send someone to town with him.'

Beeman went to his desk for a pencil and paper. 'Draw me his brand,' he said, and looked over the rangeboss's shoulder as Moore made the drawing. When he tossed down the pencil he added something else. 'Just out of mean curiosity I back-tracked as best I could. He's a shod horse, Gil, otherwise it would have been impossible. All our loose-stock has the shoes pulled before they're turned out.'

'How far could you back-track him?'

Moore smiled. 'Into the foothills. When I got into the pine and fir needles I had to give up. I'm no In'ian … Where I quit his tracks was coming downhill from the northeast.'

When Moore stopped speaking he continued to

gaze at the town marshal. Beeman understood the look and the implication without commenting. He offered Moore coffee but the rangeboss had brought the ranch supply wagon with him, it was parked in front of the general store and he had to get back over there because the rider he'd brought with him and the storekeeper might have everything loaded by now.

Beeman went to the door with Moore, thanked him and returned to the cell-room with the piece of paper. The prisoner had finished his meal but not the coffee. He held the little bucket up as he squinted at the paper Marshal Beeman was holding up outside the cell.

The prisoner nodded. 'All right. What about it?'

'Ever see it before?' Beeman asked.

The prisoner drank some coffee before replying. 'Yeah. Both their horses got that mark on the left shoulder. You found one of their horses?'

'No. But a cowman's got him out with his loose-stock. Too lame to lead to town.' Beeman folded the paper, pocketed it and leaned looking in at the man with the coffee bucket in his hand. 'All that stuff you told me last night might jibe, friend, so I'd like to try you out on something else.'

'Shoot,' the prisoner said. 'If I can help I will. But there's one thing maybe we'd ought to talk about before we get all tied up with a lot of palavering. I don't know which post General Wheeler went to inspect down south so I got no idea how far it is from Titusville. In other words, Marshal, I got no idea when he'll be arriving back up here, and if there are bushwhacking sites along the southerly route like there are on the northerly route, we could be discussing the fine points of his brother's difficulties and the other one, the man who calls himself Amos Pierson, could be selecting the best place to blast hell out of Joe Wheeler's stage.'

Gil Beeman did not dispute any of this, nor the implication that steps ought to be taken to find that other dark killer, but neither did he let it over-ride what had been on his mind before the prisoner started talking about Joe Wheeler.

Gil said, 'That feller you call Amos Pierson – I got no name for him at all – took his horse out in the night and didn't return him until late the next morning. And last night I didn't go down to the south end of town to find out if he went riding again, but I'll bet he did because although he'd locked the door to his room at the hotel from the inside, he was not in the room an' the window was wide open.'

The prisoner started to speak but Marshal Beeman held up a hand to silence him. 'Let me finish. I knew there had to be two of them the evening of the robbery because the liveryman identified a horse someone had brought back to town that night as the animal the dead man owned.'

The prisoner blandly said, 'There is no riddle there, Marshal. You just said some cowman found one of the horses lamed-up. Well, that had to be the animal the surviving brother ran away on after he saw me. He was reckless, crippled it in the rocks, turned it loose, went back and got the one I left tied where I re-loaded, and rode that horse to town after nightfall.'

Gil gazed at his prisoner. 'All right. After you re-loaded did you go back to your own animal and head for town?'

'Yes.'

'Well now, mister, it don't seem reasonable to me that a man who'd just found a horse tied among some trees would walk away and leave the animal tied an' convenient in case a bushwhacker had to come back for another horse.'

The hazel-eyed man stared for a moment before finishing the coffee and leaning to put the bucket on the cot which was on his right side. As he was straightening up he wagged his head. 'Marshal, I didn't come straight back to Titusville. I went looking for the one that got away. I figured to come back for the tied horse, maybe in the morning, but right then, while the trail was hot, I wanted to catch the other one.'

'And you didn't.'

'I didn't even see him. He must have ridden that lame horse awfully fast and hard. It was still daylight. I could see southward over miles of open country. He wasn't out there. No one was. That meant he'd stayed among the trees and rocks … until he lamed-up the horse.'

'An' you didn't go back for the tethered horse.'

'After nightfall, no. I headed for town.'

'When you got here did you look among the stalls

down yonder to see if the horse was there?'

The prisoner replied matter-of-factly. 'It couldn't be down there. I left it tied to a tree up yonder. No, I didn't look in any of the stalls. I was dog-tired and bedded down.'

Beeman straightened up off the steel bars as he drily said, 'You should have looked,' and left the prisoner gazing after him as he returned to the office, threw down his hat, rattled the coffee pot, found it half-full and stoked up a fire beneath it before going to his desk to sit down and roll his eyes.

He had no time to do anything else. Dorothy Freeman walked in. They exchanged a look before the handsome widow spoke. 'Doctor Wood told me about the dead man and gave me the autopsy bill to present to the Council the next time it meets.'

Beeman nodded.

'He also said you were supposed to have the body taken out of the shed this morning.'

Beeman rocked forward, planted both thick arms atop the desk to lean on, and gazed dispassionately at the handsome woman. 'Dorothy, I was up last night until the small hours this morning. I got another man in my cells an' there's still another one running around out there, somewhere. Tell you what; just for the hell of it you could show your civic spirit and have a couple of your yardmen take that body out of Doc's shed. Haul it down to the carpenter an' tell him to build a box for it, then you can arrange for the burial.'

She flared up at him. 'Gil Beeman that is your job. All of it. Your contract with the Council specifically states that dead indigents shall be the responsibility –.'

'Shut up, Dorothy. I wasn't finished.'

Her mouth closed slowly, her eyes widened, she was shocked.

He continued to hold her gaze and lean on the desk. 'I said there's another out there somewhere. Unless I'm wrong as hell he's a bushwhacker. Tell me something; when does the next northbound stage come up toward town from down along the border?'

'The – next – stage?'

Gil leaned back with a rattling sigh. 'Yeah, the next stage.'

When next she spoke she did not answer his question but asked one of her own. 'Are you hinting that this bushwhacker is going to waylay another of my stages?'

'In the first place it's not the same bushwhacker. That one is up in Doc's shed. In the second place, damn it, I'm runnin' out of patience about this mess. Just answer the question – please.'

She went to a chair, sat down with both hands in her lap, and said, 'One arrived this morning about sunup. It had no passengers, just some light freight and the mail sacks.'

Gil rolled his eyes ceilingward, which she correctly interpreted as increasing exasperation, and rushed into what else she had to say.

'The next stage will reach town from down

along the border sometime this afternoon. Hopefully. Schedules on those southerly runs are hard to keep. Maybe about dusk tomorrow … Gil?'

He ignored the latent question in her mention of his name, leaned forward on the desk again and said, 'You ever hear of a man named Joe Wheeler?'

She shook her head.

'Well, neither did I until last night … I guess it was this morning. Anyway, he was the target of the man who got shot after he tried to stop your stage north of town. He'll be on the stage coming up here from down south. Dorothy, never mind why, for now anyway, but someone wants him dead. You understand?'

'… They'll try to stop the stage and kill him?'

'Something like that.'

'… I see.'

'Naw you don't. Neither do I, exactly, but I know one thing – whatever in hell else is going on, there will be an attempt made on the life of General Wheeler. That much I believe because one attempt has already been made to kill him on one of your stages. And this time I want to be out there. If I can, I want to find that assassin before the stage gets up here. Now – will you get that dead man out of Doc's shed and have him buried? Because I just don't have time to do it.'

She was gazing at the hands in her lap. They were as limp as dead birds. When her head came up and her eyes met Marshal Beeman's stare, she managed a slight smile. 'Yes. I'll take care of it.'

She arose to stand erectly in front of him. She was an extremely handsome woman. 'I never saw you angry before, Gil.'

He looked steadily at her as he too arose. 'I'm not angry, Dorothy, just disgusted down to my boot-straps. I got a man in one of my cells who has a federal marshal's badge in his pocket. He may be one. He may not be too. But he sure can spin an interestin' story, and when you walked in I was tryin' to make up my mind whether to believe him an' take him with me to hunt down this bushwhacker, or leave him here.'

'Why do you doubt him?' she asked.

He made a gesture with his hands. 'I don't know that I doubt him, but if I guess wrong and he happens to be connected some way with those damned Knights of the Golden Circle he told me about, an' I take him on a manhunt with me, I could damned well end up with a bullet in the back. I know for a fact he shoots people in the back. Accidentally or not.'

She started to speak but he waved toward the door. 'Just take care of the dead one. I'll be grateful. The whole blessed town should be grateful but it won't be. Towns never are.'

She left him standing at his desk glowering at the steel-reinforced cell-room door. She was out of his thoughts almost before she left the office.

The coffee was boiling. He drew off two cups, one for himself, one for his prisoner, and returned to the cell-room. On the way down there he spoke aloud to himself. 'Women!'

Seven
Wary Men

Douglas Hall had been fed and was now ready to go out back to the outhouse across the alley, and to the wash-stand. As Beeman unlocked the door and jerked his head, he said, 'You know these Pierces or Piersons or whatever their names are, so tell me, when they set up an ambush, what do they look for?'

As they were walking toward the office Hall replied. 'I don't know them. I just know who they are and what they do for a living. I never went after them before this mess so about all I can tell you is that the one calling himself Pierce chose a place with plenty of trees and rocks for cover, in an area where if he had to run for it, he'd still have plenty of cover.' Hall paused for Beeman to step in front and open the storeroom door which led to the back alley. As Gil was opening the door Hall also said, 'Any bushwhacker wants good cover. What's it like south of here?'

Beeman had to also unlock the alley-door after which he stepped aside for his prisoner to pass. 'No trees,' he told Hall. 'Well, not near the roadway. There are jumbles of big rocks though.'

'Close to the road? Where's the soap?'

'In a few places fairly close to the road. It's under that upended coffee tin.' Beeman watched the prisoner fill the tin wash basin and go to work with the soap as he also said, 'The trouble isn't so much findin' some place Pierson can hole up an' be invisible and still be within gun-range of the road. The trouble is that it's grass-country south of town all the way to the far mountains, an' if he's hiding down there somewhere, he'll see a rider long before the rider can figure out where he is.'

Hall's reply to that was brusque. It was also a little unintelligible because he was shaving with his mouth pulled to one side. 'You're a disappointment to me, Mister Beeman. No one with the sense Gawd gave a goose rides out in broad daylight in open country searching for a forted-up bushwhacker.'

Gil leaned on the porch scowling. 'No? I can't wait for nightfall. Wheeler's coach will be along in the afternoon. Maybe a little later. Maybe at dusk but sure as hell not after nightfall.'

Hall was rinsing a face scratched and tender from using the jailhouse razor and squinted at his reflection in the cracked mirror above the wash stand when he replied, 'When was the last time anyone ran this razorblade over a stone?'

Beeman did not answer.

The prisoner turned. 'Have you ever flushed a bushwhacker before?' He allowed Beeman no opportunity to reply. 'That's what caused the army to take so many casualties back during the In'ian wars; everybody lined up in regimental front with the flag out ahead while the redskins were flat in the grass, behind trees, down in gullies ....' He smiled at Marshal Beeman who was regarding him dourly. 'We'll go down the road in a wagon behind a team and maybe with some junk piled in the wagon-bed like we're peddlers or tinkers. Can you get a wagon?'

Gil jerked his head for Hall to pass him and return to the office. He locked each door behind his prisoner. When they were inside Beeman rattled the coffee pot. It was nearly empty so he did not bother stoking up the stove or dropping another fistful of ground beans into the pot, he went to his desk, sat down and pointed to the wall-bench. After the prisoner was seated he said, 'Yeah, I've gone after a few bushwhackers. Maybe not as many as you have, but that other one, the man calling himself Pierce, wasn't any great shakes at it.'

'He might have been, Mister Beeman, if I hadn't been behind him. This other one knows someone is trying to run him down. He's not goin' to be as easy as Pierce was. Can you get an old wagon and fix it to look like we're a pair of peddlers?'

Beeman didn't say whether he could or not, he took his prisoner back to his cell, locked him in and without another word between them, let Hall regard his broad back as he returned to the office where he flung aside the keyring and walked out of the jailhouse hiking southward.

Hall's assurance irked him. So did something else; Hall's assumption that they would do this together, which was not something Gil had not thought of but he had made no decision about it and, as he'd speculated during Dorothy Freeman's visit, if Hall was not everything he had said he was, Beeman might never get back to Titusville standing up.

The first question he had for the liveryman was whether that disappearing damned horse was in his stall. Hamelin shook his head. 'Nope. He was snuck out again some time last night and ain't been brought back.'

If the liveryman expected this revelation to encourage a lengthy discussion he was disappointed. Marshal Beeman asked if he had an old wagon he could hire out, and some boxes and loose hay, maybe a few saddles and other items which could pass for trading goods he could put in the wagon.

Hamelin stared, but only briefly, then he nodded his head. 'You don't want to look like what you are. Sure, I can make up an outfit for you. When you want it?'

'As soon as you can make it up. And Stan; not a damned word.'

Hamelin smiled broadly. 'Marshal, you got no idea how many secrets'll go into the grave with me.'

Gil gazed at the older man for a moment. 'But I

can guess,' he said, and returned to the roadway.

This time he walked the full length of town and
entered the hotel as the proprietor was sweeping
the hallway and raised sulphurous eyes. 'Why is
it,' he asked whiningly, 'that every blessed time I
sweep this hall, someone walks in and tracks the
dirt back where it was?' He leaned on the broom.
'You never returned the key, Marshal.'

Beeman started past. 'I want to use it one
more time, then you can have it back.'

The hotelman turned, still leaning on his
broom, to watch Beeman return to the locked door
of the room he had entered last night to find it
empty with the window open. When Beeman
entered this time the old man's curiosity got the
better of him. He went up as far as the door to
peer inside.

The lawman did not have to search, nor was he
surprised that Pierson's saddlebags and other
personal articles were not there.

The hotelman was not surprised either as he
made his assessment from the doorway. 'At least
this time when one of 'em slipped away he'd paid
up in advance ... Who is he, Marshal? Member of
some outlaw band?'

Beeman stepped back to the hallway, handed
over the key, shook his head and marched back
out to the roadway with the old man glaring after
him and muttering uncomplimentary remarks.

Down in front of the stage company's corralyard
a pair of patient mules hitched to a spring wagon
stood near the gateway as three yardmen loaded

something wrapped in old canvas like a cocoon. Beeman slackened his pace but Dorothy saw him anyway when she came out behind the yardmen. He would have cut quickly across the road in the direction of the saloon but she called to him before he could do that.

'Marshal?'

Gil went on down there, nodded to her and turned to watch one of her hostlers climb to the wagon seat while the other two went stoically back to work in the yard.

'The carpenter is waiting.' she told him, as the wagon moved away, 'and Mister Lipton dragooned several of those old men who live at the lower end of town to go out to the cemetery and dig the hole.' When he faced back she was faintly smiling at him. 'None of it any cost to the town. My civic duty, I think you called it.'

He nodded at her, expressionless and impatient. He still hadn't made a decision about his prisoner, and by now Stan Hamelin would about have that wagon rigged out. 'Titusville will be grateful, Dorothy.'

She put her head slightly on one side, still faintly smiling at him. 'But it won't be. That's what you said, isn't it?'

He stared at her. *Women. If they aren't making everything sound like a question, they're playing games!*

'What about your prisoner, are you going to take him with you on your manhunt for the second bushwhacker?'

'I don't know.'

'Well, take someone. My yard boss is –.'

'Dorothy, your yardboss hasn't drawn a completely sober breath in years.'

Her smile faded, some of the other Dorothy Freeman appeared. 'He's worked for me since I took over the franchise and I've never seen him drunk!'

'I didn't say drunk, I said stone-sober. Did you ever smell his breath?'

She reddened. 'Of course not!'

'Well, I have, and a few times before breakfast. He gets an early start. It's nothing against him. I've known a lot of men who for one reason or another couldn't get cranked up after they got out of bed without a boost, an' that's fine with me. But not when guns might be involved along with plumb sober judgement. Excuse me.'

He left her staring after him as he returned to the jailhouse office, removed a pair of Winchesters from the wall-rack, put extra loads for each gun in a coat pocket, then left the weapons and the coat near the roadway door as he went back down to the only occupied cell where the prisoner was lying on his cot, ankles crossed and both hands clasped under his head. He eyed the big lawman dispassionately, and waited.

Beeman was curt. 'Mister Hall, you're goin' to set on the wagon seat with me with your belt-gun buckled on, with the gun empty, and with a pair of carbines on the plankin' at our feet. And Mister Hall, if you so much as scratch inside your shirt while we're drivin' along, I'll blow you out of your pants.'

The other tall man continued to lie relaxed looking at Gil Beeman. 'You got the rig ready?'

'It will be by the time we get down there. Get up.'

Hall did not move except to free one hand from beneath his head to swipe at a circling fly. 'Maybe you'd ought to take someone else,' he told Beeman. 'I got to explain that I don't care whether I get Pierson before he kills General Wheeler, or someone else gets him first. And right now, listening to you and looking at you, my impression is that whether you belong to The Golden Circle or not, I might be in a hell of a lot more peril from you than from Pierson. I think I'll stay here.'

Beeman leaned on the opened cell door. 'I admire a man being straight-out with me, Mister Hall. But right now my problem is that I don't have a lot of time to go all over hell tryin' to find someone else. That stagecoach is raisin' dust down there somewhere. You understand?'

Hall removed both hands from beneath his head, came up into a sitting position on the side of the bunk and while gazing at the dented lard pail which served as a jailhouse commode pot, he wagged his head. 'It doesn't take two men, Marshal. I proved that up yonder where I shot the other one.' He finally turned his face toward Beeman. 'My chances of coming back to town sitting up are two-to-one against. *You* understand?'

Hall arose and stretched before walking a little closer to the blocked doorway. Beeman eyed him coldly. 'I'll do it alone,' he growled and stepped back into the little hallway, turned and slammed the steel door. As he was inserting the key to lock it, Douglas Hall said, 'You probably could, but I know for a fact, Marshal, that two men can sneak up on a bushwhacker a lot easier than one man can. How about that pot-bellied liveryman? Or maybe the feller who runs the saloon, an' who hasn't done a lick of hard work in twenty years? Or how about that old man who has the gunshop? He's long in the tooth but if it was me I'd prefer him to the other pair.'

Gil straightened up with his hand ready to twist the key. 'Just what is it you're up to?' he asked, still without cranking the key.

'What I'm up to, Marshal, is my gun will be loaded, so will the carbine, and whatever happens you think, really think, before you point a gun at me, because if my suspicions about you are as bad as yours are about me, all you got to do is look like you want to aim at me, an' unless you're awful damned fast I'll kill you.' For a moment Hall's expression remained fixed and hard, then his face relaxed as he went on speaking. 'If we're both wrong about each other, and I've begun to figure that's very possible, why then, Mister Beeman, I think we might make a pretty good team.' Hall glanced at the hand on the key. 'Twist it or cut bait.'

Gil Beeman withdrew the key, pocketed it, yanked the door open and jerked his head.

Up in the office he armed his prisoner and stood stoically watching Hall load his sixgun and drop it back into its holster. As Beeman handed Hall one of the Winchesters he said, 'It's loaded. Take the old coat off the wall and let's walk down the back alley.' He showed a mirthless grin. 'It's not that I believe there are any of your Knights of the Golden Circle in Titusville, it's just that if we go down the alley no one's likely to see that I let my prisoner out.'

When they reached the rear door Hall made his own comment about that. 'Yeah. That would take a lot of explaining, wouldn't it?'

Beeman ignored that. As they were walking, heat struck them. Muggy heat. Beeman looked upwards. There were huge clouds with soiled edges moving with infinite slowness from beyond the northeasterly mountains. It looked like the stockmen were going to get their downpour after all.

Hall also raised his eyes. 'Be a couple of days yet,' he opinioned. 'At least in any country I've been in clouds moving that slow take a long time to get anywhere and unload.'

Beeman did not pursue the topic. He was already thinking of the country they would traverse, selecting and sometimes discarding sites where a bushwhacker might be.

If the man had a carbine, which he certainly did have, he could hide farther from the road than if all he had was a handgun. For this kind of an ambush no seasoned killer would not have a long-barrelled weapon.

When they entered Hamelin's barn from out back the wagon and hitch were up near the front of the runway, ready and waiting. Stan Hamelin and his dayman were standing beside the rig smiling from ear to ear like very satisfied fellow-conspirators.

Eight
Caught!

The team broke a sweat before Beeman and Hall had covered a mile. It was that kind of weather. Those big old soiled-looking clouds appeared not to have moved an inch, but that was probably an illusion. The air was still and heavy as Douglas Hall mopped his neck and squinted out over the countryside on both sides and dead ahead.

The wagon had an assortment of items piled in careless disarray behind and below the spring-seat. Hall twisted to examine the load, and laughed as he faced forward. 'I don't know what we look like, traders, wagon-tramps or thieves. There's everything back there but a stove.'

Beeman said nothing. He knew this country, had been up and down the road dozens of times and had also ridden the range on both sides, but never with any idea of considering it from the standpoint of an ambush, which was the way he was studying it now.

As he had told Hall, while there were stands of timber they were in isolated, distant areas. But there were fields of rocks close to the road as well as farther out on both sides.

It would be the rocks, he told himself. There was little else a bushwhacker could use for cover while he waited.

Hall broke into the marshal's reverie. 'He's no greenhorn. He won't be close to town. Even at a fair distance the sound of gunfire would carry quite a ways.'

Beeman nodded, shook off sweat and jutted his jaw ahead where the land seemed to undulate from heat-haze. 'Five, six miles along the rocks are closer together. Up there he can find little erosion gullies to hide his horse in.'

The horses plodded effortlessly, sweating from the humidity and heat, not from the load because the liveryman had not piled anything into the wagon-bed that had much weight to it.

Hall rolled a smoke, lit up and offered the makings to Gil Beeman, who shook his head as he said, 'I like the smell but twice when I tried it, I got sick.'

Hall smiled understandingly. 'Yeah. I did too, but I wouldn't let something as small as a quirley bluff me out.' He laughed and Beeman smiled. 'I didn't have the guts to stick it out,' he told Hall. 'Look beneath the seat. Maybe the liveryman put a canteen under there.'

He had, but evidently he'd put it there a long time ago because the water tasted stale. But it was wet.

Hall wondered about their sweating team. Beeman jutted his jaw again. 'There's a stone trough a mile or so ahead where the lady who owns the local stageline had her men make a turn-out.'

Hall removed his smoke and looked at Beeman. 'A lady owns the stageline?'

'Yeah. Her husband drove for the earlier owner until he got buried under a landslide. She bought out the owner not long afterwards.'

Douglas Hall smoked, watched the country for a while, regarded his companion's profile for a moment then said, 'She must be a tough old buzzard.'

Gil leaned back, re-set his hat lower to protect his eyes from the bounce-back of sunlight and shook his head. 'She's tough an' she's blunt, but she's a hell of a good lookin' woman.'

'Never re-married?'

'No. To tell you the truth, Mister Hall, handsome though she sure as hell is, she's intimidatin' as hell.'

The federal officer killed his smoke and was silent for a long time. The next time he spoke they had the stone trough in sight. As far as he could see there was no creek up there and he was interested in the source of water that trickled over one end of the trough making a respectable mud-hole in front where drinking horses would stand. 'Where's the water come from?' he asked, as Gil began angling wide so that when he came up to the trough both horses would be facing it as he replied,

'From directly beneath the trough.'

Hall was impressed. 'Sump spring?'

Beeman had the horses aimed right but had to haul back a little because the animals were thirsty. He set the binders, climbed down to remove the bridles before the animals drank to prevent them from sucking air with the water as they drank.

Hall helped. While they were standing with the horses Hall squinted southward, but if he expected to see dust he was disappointed, the land was full of silence, emptiness, and lack of movement. He asked if Gil knew what time it was. But neither of them carried a pocket watch so Beeman had to make a guess based on the position of the sun. 'Early afternoon,' he replied. 'We might not see any dust for another three, four hours.'

Hall was leaning against the stone trough facing eastward. There were mud-daubers flying some kind of pattern. The arrival of men and horses had upset them. They did not make any serious attempts to sting but they were clearly in a bad mood because earth-bound critters were obstructing the mud which they gathered to make nests from.

Hall swung his hat a couple of times when the insects got too close, and the second time he did this he stepped to the north end of the trough. Beeman was ready to re-bridle the horse nearest him when Hall said, 'Well, well, well. Look on the far side, Marshal. Someone riding a shod horse stopped here. Must have been some time ago. The tracks close to the trough have dissolved but the ones farther back ... See them?'

Gil walked around in back and nodded. 'Could have been anyone. It could have been Pierson last night or early this morning.' He turned to trace out the direction the rider had taken when he'd left the trough. It was southward on an angling course back to the road. Out there, it was barely possible to make out tracks, and if the shod horse hadn't had muddy feet which left definite imprints, it would have been impossible to pick those tracks from the dozens of other tracks on what was a well-used road.

When they were hauling around to resume their southward journey nothing was said between them for as long as they could make out the tracks. After that Gil gauged the onward country from narrowed eyes looking for jumbles of large rocks which were near the road.

'Up ahead somewhere,' he conjectured. Hall said nothing. He was leaning forward a little. They passed two areas where ancient rocks, several nearly as tall as a mounted man, would have made ideal sites for an ambush. Except for one thing: There was no place near them to hide a horse.

Beeman settled back on the seat. He was now more interested in the arrow-straight roadway far ahead. Dorothy Freeman had been vague about when this particular coach would appear, but that did not particularly bother Gil. What mattered was that it *would appear*.

His feeling was that regardless of the stillness, the emptiness and the great depth of silence, he was moving steadily toward some kind of violent apex, and that inclined him to speculate a little about something he had not considered before.

Suppose the stage did show up, and suppose he and his companion found the bushwhacker and there was a fight, which was very likely about the time the stage arrived. Those three men who were passengers had blazed away the other time they'd encountered trouble, and they might do so again, in which case somebody could damned well get hurt.

He looked at Douglas Hall. 'How do you feel about gettin' caught in the middle?'

Hall was mopping off sweat again. 'About the same as anyone in their right mind would feel. Worried.' He stowed the soggy bandana. 'If we don't find Pierson before we see the stage coming, and he opens up like his brother tried to do up north, and we're sitting out here on our horses, how would those men in the coach know we're not part of the ambush?' As he finished making this statement, he pointed. 'There. The field of big boulders on the left. There's an arroyo behind it. It's just about the right distance from the town and back maybe a mile is a stand of trees.' Hall lowered his arm. 'Marshal, if I was a bushwhacker that's the place I'd pick.'

Gil again re-set his hat. The sun was behind them, still high but some distance from the meridian. Even so its brilliance was reflected off every minuscule piece of mica in roadway dust.

That arroyo angled. It also ran past the place

Beeman pointed out and continued southward out of sight southward. The farther it went, the closer it came to providing additional places to hide a horse near other piles of man-high rocks.

Gil spat over the side, straightened up and returned his attention to the place Hall had indicated. It was the first, and nearest, of several excellent ambushing sites. Gil cocked his head to locate the sun, then began angling toward the rocks as he spoke in a louder tone of voice. 'Time to rest. I'm hungry. How about you?'

Hall returned his gaze from the rocks to Marshal Beeman. In a quieter tone he said, 'He may not recognise me from up where I shot his brother, but sure as hell he'll recognise you. Outlaws don't ride into a town and take a room there without making a point of looking up the local law.'

Beeman was slackening the lines as they got close to the tumbled mass of large rocks. 'I never said we'd ride up on his blind side, Mister Hall.' He stopped the team and jumped to the ground. But he kept his back to the rocks as did Douglas Hall.

There was no food nor had Beeman expected Hamelin to have had that much foresight, so he dug into the load until he found a fairly small box, and started to back away from the wagon with it as he said, 'Slip their bridles so's they can pick grass. Be sure to hobble them.'

Hall worked with his back to the rocks. He did not even look over his shoulder to see where Gil Beeman had gone with the little box. When he finished hobbling and was straightening up, he fished out the soggy bandana and mopped his face with it as he turned toward the rocks and walked in Beeman's direction.

Several of the boulders were clumped so close together there was no way to see behind them. Other rocks, about half as massive, lay on both sides.

Beeman put down the box, turned very carefully and turned back as he spoke loudly again. 'Did you ever make sense out of all the talk back up in that town?' He did not give Hall a chance to speak. 'Nobody seemed to know what they was doing. And that barman's story about a bunch of soldiers comin' north with the stagecoach … What in hell was all that about?'

Douglas Hall was squatting in full sunshine. Whatever shade was down here, was on the far side of the rocks. He did not even hesitate. 'Maybe there's a shipment of bullion on that stage. Maybe an army payroll or somethin' like that.' Hall went a little farther. 'You goin' to hog all that dried beef? Where's the canteen? A man can sweat out water in this damned country as fast as he takes it in.'

Beeman looked at his companion with a twinkle. Hall hadn't had any idea what the town marshal was going to do here, but he'd had sufficient presence of mind to go along with it. For the first time since Gil Beeman had encountered Douglas Hall, he felt a faint stirring of approval. One thing was finally evident; whatever else Hall might be up to, he sure as hell was no friend of the man they were hunting, and that, at least for the time being, was all that concerned the Titusville town marshal.

Silence fell between them. Beeman sat on the little box. His companion rolled and lit a smoke. The horses pulled the wagon in short jerks and halts as they pursued their quest for grass-heads.

As time passed Beeman sorted through a number of excuses for going around behind the rank of big rocks, decided on the most reasonable one and arose with a grunt as he said, 'Be back directly.'

Hall stubbed out his quirley, unwound up to his full height acting as though he might remonstrate, but in the end he said nothing as Gil stepped around the loose rocks north of the big ones and passed from sight.

It was a bad ten minutes for Douglas Hall. There was a diversion when the horses stopped cropping feed and raised their heads looking southward, ears forward to indicate total concentration.

Hall moved quickly away from the rocks so he would have an uninterrupted sighting down the road, and sure enough there was dust. The horses had probably also picked up sound. They would hardly have noticed just the dust when they threw up their heads.

It did not occur to Hall that whatever lay below that dust might not be General Wheeler's stagecoach, which was due from the south, would be raising dust, and would arrive where Hall was standing within about a half hour.

He turned back towards the rocks – and froze in his tracks.

Marshal Beeman was standing there with an empty holster. Behind him was a darker man, slightly built, somewhat shorter than Beeman, and holding two sixguns in his hands, one of which he had taken from the lawman.

Beeman was looking straight at Hall, expressionless, slightly flushed in the face, and with sucked-flat lips.

The dark man was staring at Douglas Hall. For seconds he did not seem to be breathing. He appeared to be trying very hard to place a face he thought he had seen somewhere before. There was uncertainty in his expression, for a while anyway.

He had been in hiding when Marshal Beeman came picking his way around behind the rank of large boulders facing the road. He had not expected the town marshal and perhaps for that reason had not recognised him immediately. But, when he did recognise him, he simply had to palm his gun in the shadows, arise and as Beeman inched past being careful of rocks, extend his arm and quietly hiss.

But he had no idea Marshal Beeman of Titusville being down here in a trader's wagon with a companion was part of a conspiracy to catch him until he finally placed the face of the lawman's companion.

The bushwhacker stood for close on ten seconds staring at Beeman's companion before he said, 'By Gawd I know you. You were up north in the rocks. Up where my brother got killed.'

Hall took a desperate chance. 'That was your brother? Yeah, I was up yonder when someone tried to stop the coach and everyone inside it opened up on him.'

Gil Beeman was facing in Hall's direction. The man was doing a passable job of acting. He was, Beeman knew, banking on the fact that while the bushwhacker had finally recognised Hall as having been present when his brother had been killed, had initially mistaken him for his brother and after discovering his mistake had rolled off his vantage place and fled, he had been fleeing when his brother had been killed and did not know who had actually done the killing.

For Hall's sake as well as his own, he hoped Hall had sounded convincing to the dark man behind him with a sixgun in each hand.

Nine
The Oncoming Dust

But the dark man remained in place, guns poised, clearly endeavouring to make some sense out of what had to be an event full of unique contradictions to him.

When he finally spoke, addressing Douglas Hall, there was an edge to his voice. 'You had a Winchester,' he said, 'and you was behind us.'

Hall shrugged about that. 'I was hunting.'

The dark man stood in silence for a long moment, then cocked his head. Without mentioning what had alerted him to approaching travellers he jerked his head. 'Back around behind the rocks. You – toss that gun away and walk behind the lawman.'

Hall obeyed. The killer herded them like sheep until they were hidden, then he leathered his own weapon and cocked Beeman's gun as he said, 'Squat down an' don't make a sound.'

The captives sank to the ground. The noise from

the roadway was louder, but muffled to some extent by the intervening rocks. Hall's steady regard of the assassin brought a snarl as the dark man leaned against one of the tall rocks. 'What're you starin' at?'

'You. I remember, as I was coming down towards the stageroad someone was perched atop of a rock looking down there. Was that you?'

The dark man glared for a moment before replying. 'Yeah. It was me.' He cocked Beeman's handgun and pointed it squarely at Hall. 'You was stalkin' us. You wasn't huntin' up there.'

Beeman was watching the finger curled inside the triggerguard of his sixgun. It did not seem to be tightening. He spoke to the bushwhacker quietly. 'Whoever's coming will hear the shot.'

The killer swung his attention to the marshal. 'That wagon loaded with junk ... You two bastards was lookin' for me an' that was to make me think you were just travellers. Marshal, who is this friend of yours?'

Beeman answered in the same quiet tone. 'A local pot-hunter. He peddles game meat around town.'

The dark man sneered again, but not altogether convincingly. 'Maybe.' He faced Hall again. 'You was still back there when the shootin' started. What happened to my brother?'

'He got shot in the back.'

'Where were you?'

'Trying to keep down.'

'Did you see which of them killed him?'

'From inside the stagecoach? I couldn't make out anyone in there for gunfire.'

The dark man's gunhand relaxed a trifle. 'It don't matter. They'll be along directly an' this time it'll be done right. I got an ivory bead on the front sight of my Winchester. It's supposed to make it easier to aim in the dark, but all I need it for now is to shoot the lead horse. That'll stop the stage.'

Beeman drily said, 'It will most likely up-end if it's travelling fast.'

The dark man bared his teeth in a cold smile. 'I hope so. I wanted one man on there, but now I want all three of them ... What did you say about soldiers ridin' with the coach?'

Hall answered. 'That's what I heard up in Titusville. A soldier escort. I thought maybe there was a load of money on the coach.'

The dark man continued to stare at them while he seemed to be turning something over in his mind. He finally gestured with the gun. 'Flat down with your arms in back.'

They obeyed, he lashed their wrists and ankles then rolled them face-up with a boot toe. He flung Marshal Beeman's gun away and stood a moment listening before turning to edge around the big rocks where he would have a view of the southward road.

He remained like that for several minutes before pulling back and turning. His face twisted. 'Horsemen,' he told them, moving to the leaning Winchester against the rock. 'Six of them.

Goddamit they're goin' to see your wagon and team out there.'

Gil Beeman let all his breath out very slowly. It wasn't General Wheeler's stage after all. He looked at Douglas Hall, who was staring at the dark man, evidently trying to anticipate what he might do.

But if Hall expected the outlaw to react to the approach of riders with confusion, he was disappointed. He stepped over to Gil Beeman, took his badge, pinned it on his own shirt, hooked the Winchester into the crook of one arm and turned, but before he moved around in front of the rocks he offered a warning. 'Either one of you open your mouths and I'll blow the tops off your heads.'

He disappeared around the rocks and took up a slouching position near the wagon, holding the carbine loosely as the horsemen came up close enough to see him and the wagon with its team.

A large, fully bearded man shouted and raised his right hand in a salute. The killer raised his right hand the same way. He may have hoped the horsemen were in a hurry and would ride on by, but at best that could have been a very feeble hope. People travelling through invariably stopped when they met someone, if for no other reason than to ask directions.

The big bearded man reined toward the wagon with his companions behind him. When he stopped he sat a moment considering what he saw, the wagon, its nondescript load, the bridle-less team and the dark man leaning on the wagon's far side with a Winchester showing.

The bearded man raised a limp cuff to push sweat off his face and said, 'Howdy. You in trouble? Wagon broke down?'

Pierson smiled back. 'No trouble. It's too hot to keep goin' for a while.'

The bearded man's little blue eyes moved constantly. He leaned, spat tobacco juice and said, 'Where are your partners?'

Pierson hung fire. '... They're around the back in the shade.'

The big man jutted his jaw. 'Someone lost their sixgun,' he said, indicating the gun Pierson had ordered Hall to throw away.

The outlaw turned, saw the gun and turned back. He was looking squarely into the muzzle of the big man's sixgun. His hand tightened on the Winchester. Other handguns appeared behind the bearded man. Pierson smiled and tapped the badge on his shirt. 'Fact is, I been on the trail of a pair of outlaws. This is their wagon.'

The bearded man's aimed gun did not waver. 'Where are they?' he asked, and when Pierson jerked his head the big man swung to the ground. Around him the other horsemen also dismounted. The big man did not look away from the bushwhacker as he spoke to his companions. 'Couple of you boys go look behind them rocks.'

As a pair of riders moved to obey Pierson continued to force a smile while looking straight at the large, bearded man. 'They're goin' to lie to high heaven,' he said.

The big man accepted that. 'I expect so. You're

the marshal of some town up north?'

'Titusville. It's about ten miles north. Who are you?'

'Grant Herlong. Free-grazer. These gents work for me. We free-graze up through this part of the country every spring after we contract cattle on a weight-gain basis. We thought maybe we'd have a look around up here before we moved the cattle north.' Grant Herlong stopped speaking when his riders came around from behind the rocks with Gil Beeman and the federal marshal. He stared, spat, and faced Pierson as he said, 'Tell you what, Marshal; you drop that Winchester and toss down your handgun an' we'll talk.' There were guns in the hands of the rough-looking rangemen standing on either side and slightly to the rear of the big man. Pierson sighed, dropped his weapons and was turning when Beeman said, 'Two years ago wasn't it?'

Herlong regarded the only man among them as large and thick as he was, and nodded his head. 'Yeah. But you couldn't have flung me out of that saloon if I'd been sober ... What the hell is goin' on here, Marshal? For a minute there I thought maybe you'd rode on and this feller was the new Titusville lawman. Y'know how I knew he wasn't? The town's fifteen miles up the road, not ten miles.'

Beeman rubbed his wrists as he regarded Pierson. When he was ready he told the rangemen what Pierson had been hiding in the rocks to do, and when he mentioned who was on the stagecoach, two of Herlong's rangemen glared and one of them spoke in a heavy drawl. 'That's a fact? That turn-coat son of a bitch is out here? Comin' up this damned road?'

Grant Herlong turned. 'What's the matter with you?' he snarled at the faded, leathery-hided rider. 'You know this general?'

'Know him? Grant, that there's the Secesh gen'el that went an' took an oath to the Yankees after the war an' where I come from, they'd hang him so high if they could catch the old bastard birds'd be able to make nests in his hair.'

Herlong gazed at his rider, then spat and looked at the other riders. Only one other man showed rancour in his face but he remained quiet. Herlong said, 'For hell's sake, Luther, that war's been over an' done with for twenty years. What's the matter with you anyway?' Herlong faced back towards Gil Beeman, glanced at Douglas Hall, over to Pierson and back to Hall. 'I don't mean no offence,' he said. 'Just who the hell are you?'

Hall fished out his little badge. They all stared at it. Herlong cleared his throat as he shot a sudden stabbing stare at one of his riders. 'Well now, Mister Marshal,' he said to Hall. 'We sort of fished you out of a rainbarrel, so to speak. If the greasy-lookin' individual is all Marshal Beeman said he is, why if we hadn't come along he'd most likely have killed you.'

Beeman looked at Hall. They had both seen the look the cowman had shot at one of his men. Hall did not look at the rider, he looked squarely back at the big bearded man. 'I think you're right, Mister Herlong, and that means I owe you one.'

Herlong sighed, winked and said, 'You remember that, Marshal. Now then, gents, suppose we bridle them horses on the wagon and – where is this bushwhacker's horse?' One of the men who had gone behind the rocks to free the pair of lawmen spoke up. 'There's a saddle animal down in a gully back yonder a few yards.'

Herlong said, 'Go fetch it up here, will you?' He looked at Pierson for a moment then asked a question. 'You want this Secesh soldier for some personal reason, do you?'

Hall spoke first. 'No. He was hired to kill him. Him and his brother. I shagged them for a month, was coming up onto them when they were in position to bushwhack the general on his way south ....'

'They didn't do it?' Herlong asked.

'One tried. He got killed. This one tucked tail and ran, and now he's down here to try again, only this time he mostly wants revenge for the killing of his brother.'

Herlong hooked meaty thumbs in his shellbelt and watched his man return leading a saddled horse. Beeman watched for the left shoulder until he saw the brand Chief Moore had drawn for him, then he was turning away when Pierson suddenly screamed at Hall.

'*You* killed him! Hunter! Yeah you were a hunter! A damned manhunter! I wish I'd searched you an' found that badge. You'd be dyin' gutshot for a damned week before you got it done!'

He was poised, tight-wound as a spring when Gil Beeman moved ahead and pointed a finger at the wildly enraged dark man. 'That's enough.' He stood a moment waiting, and turned away only when he thought the danger of a personal attack had passed.

It might not have if one of Herlong's riders hadn't yelled causing a distraction. 'Yonder! There's a stage coming!'

Everyone turned except Marshal Hall who had retrieved his sixgun. He faced the bushwhacker and stood like a stone glaring back.

Pierson did no more than glare but his face was scarlet and beaded with fresh sweat.

The oncoming coach was a large vehicle, larger than was usually used on a flat-country run, and it had six horses on the pole instead of two. There was an armed man on the box beside the driver and dusty luggage lashed on top. It was the armed guard who saw the crowd of men standing close to the rocks with a wagon in front of them and shifted his rifle from between his knees to his lap, holding it in both hands. The driver responded to something the gunguard said by looking quickly to his left, then hollered up his hitch into a run and leaned into the wind this brought against him.

None of the men on foot moved. Instinctive prudence kept them motionless, hands away from their weapons as the coach bucketed towards them trailing ten-foot banners of dun dust.

Not a word was spoken. Those two former Confederates among the free-grazers watched malevolently. Every man over near the rocks on the east side of the road was trying to catch a glimpse of the passengers.

There were two of them, one beefy and fairly young, the other smaller, much older with a scraggly grey beard. They both wore stained campaign hats and when they leaned to look out at the men near the rocks, the older man put his arm in a tentative salute. Beeman, Hill, Herlong and most of the other watching men waved back. Two of Herlong's riders did not and neither did Pierson. Of the three men who did not wave back the one with the fiercest expression was not either of the former rebel soldiers, it was the man calling himself Amos Pierson.

The coach sped past, dust began to settle, Beeman blew out a big breath and faced the dark man. 'Pull up your pantslegs,' he said.

Pierson had an under-and-over .41 calibre hideout pistol in one boot-top. Beeman took it and spun the bushwhacker around, roughly searched him, removed a wicked-bladed knife from a shoulder sheath and pushed his prisoner toward the saddled horse.

The horsemen waited until the team had been bridled, the two lawmen were on the spring-seat, then mounted and started northward where the distant dust showed the stagecoach at least a mile ahead and widening the distance.

Grant Herlong turned back to ride with the

wagon. He had a fresh cud in his cheek and tobacco stain at the outer corners of his full beard. He rolled his eyes then laughed. It was a booming sound, the kind that brought up something to match it in the heart of everyone within hearing distance.

He looked around where his riders had Amos Pierson tightly surrounded, then leaned on the saddlehorn looking past Beeman to the federal marshal.

'You thinkin' about retiring?' he asked.

Hall's eyes widened. 'Retiring? What gave you that idea?'

Herlong eased back off the saddlehorn. 'Partner, whenever a man gets as close to bein' killed as you did back there, it's time to commence thinkin' that Someone is sendin' you a signal that He's just too damned busy to keep lookin' after you.'

Ten

A Difference Of Opinion

Grant Herlong rode to within sight of Titusville, then slapped Marshal Beeman on the back as he started to rein westward. 'We done our good deed for the day, Mister Beeman, an' now we got to get back to work.' He looked straight at the federal officer. 'Marshal, I hope you got a good memory.'

Hall looked back from an expressionless face, and nodded. 'I have, Mister Herlong. I'm obliged to you. If we don't meet again – keep your powderhorn higher'n your shot pouch.'

Herlong laughed as he left the road in a swirl of dust, accompanied by his hard-bitten riding crew. When he was a fair distance away Douglas Hall said, 'That rider of his in the checkered shirt ... Tall man with grey hair ...'

Beeman did not bother turning to seek this particular rider, he continued to look up where Titusville's rooftops were discernible in the fading afternoon daylight. 'One outlaw at a time, Mister Hall. Did you ever see him before; got any idea what he did or where he's wanted?'

Hall shook his head as he shifted his attention up ahead to the town. 'No. Like you said, one manhunt at a time ... And I sure owe Mister Herlong.'

Amos Pierson who had ridden in stony silence since his capture, looked menacingly at the federal officer. 'The law,' he growled contemptuously. 'You knew he was a wanted man, but because old whiskers saved your bacon you let him go.'

Douglas Hall considered the dark man. 'What I know, you back-shooting whelp, is that after fifteen years in this business I don't sit in judgement, that's what the courts are for, an' when a man's several hundred miles from court, out in the field doin' a job, the same rules don't always apply. I suppose one of Mister Herlong's riders is a wanted man – somewhere – but today he helped the law and that's good enough to keep me from asking a lot of questions.'

Dusk was on the way when they entered town. Beeman led off to the west-side alley because, as a result of it being supper time, Main Street was nearly empty, he preferred not having word spread that he had returned. He halted the wagon out back and got down.

Stan Hamelin was up at the cafe. His nightman was in the process of forking feed when the wagon arrived out back and now there were three men instead of two. The nightman stood stone still for seconds before leaning aside the hay fork to do what he was paid to do; take care of the animals and park the wagon.

He recognised Marshal Hall and the dark man, and while Beeman said nothing, which established the precedent for his companions who did not speak to the hostler either, the nightman did not require an explanation. He watched Hall and Beeman return to the darkening alley with the dark man between them and walk northward in the direction of the jailhouse.

When Mister Hamelin returned from the cafe, if he returned – sometimes he went home directly after supper – but if he returned this evening the nightman had something to tell him he was certain would provide his employer with the best imaginable excuse for not going directly home, not until after he had gone up to the saloon with his gossip. Up there it would be worth five or six straight shots without Hamelin having to pay.

Beeman's arrival had been noticed elsewhere because he and his companions'd had to pass among the dilapidated tarpaper-shacks at the lower end of town where those old scarecrows resided, but since their involvement with folks 'uptown' was minimal, this observation at least might not be passed along for several days.

Beeman was not actually bothered by a desire not to have been generally noticed arriving back in Titusville. He simply had preferred, as he always had, not to show up in town leading a captive. The West was full of lawmen who liked nothing better than to ride straight through the centre of their towns leading some bedraggled – or dead – outlaw on a worn-out horse.

Beeman was not one of those. When he had the lamp lighted in his office, he shed his coat and hat, sat down at the desk and pointed at the wall-bench for Amos Pierson. Douglas Hall was building a smoke. All three of them looked like they'd been yanked through a knothole, and although the subject did not arise right away, they were also hungry.

Beeman, took out his desk-bottle, took two swallows and passed it to the federal marshal, who also swallowed a couple of times then raised his eyebrows and waited for Gil Beeman's shrug before passing the bottle to Amos Pierson.

The jailhouse was still hot after a long day of intermittent sunshine and mugginess. Those dirty old cloud galleons were still drifting toward town and there was no air stirring.

Pierson surprised both law officers. After returning the bottle he said, 'You know what they're sayin' in the East? There's war comin' with the Spanish over in Cuba, and sure as hell Joe Wheeler will be in one of the field commands, an' they're sayin' this is what he's been waitin' for so's he can pay back the damned Yankees by lettin' the Spanish win.'

Gil Beeman leaned back in his chair stoically regarding the dark man, but Douglas Hall's reaction was different. As he was dousing his smoke in the sandbox around the office spittoon, he said, 'That's what the Knights of the Golden Circle are saying. No one else is and if you'd kept up on what the newspapers are reporting back east you'd know this is the truth.'

Pierson was poised to retort when Gil Beeman's interruption stopped him. 'Never mind what they're sayin' back east. We're a thousand miles from 'em. They're always sayin' something, and out here they might as well be talkin' to the man in the moon. Pierson, or whatever your name is, who hired you to waylay General Wheeler?'

This time the dark man's candidness was not forthcoming. He sat across the room, dark eyes fixed on Gil Beeman, saying nothing.

Beeman shrugged and hitched forward to lean on the desk. 'All right. I only asked that because the federal marshal will want to know. Me, all I care about is that you've upset the hell out of things in my territory, tried to murder a man, and would have likely shot me an' Marshal Hall. Attempted murder three times. I'll work up charges against you and keep you locked up until a circuit-riding judge shows up. After the court's handled you, why then I expect whatever else happens to you will be out of my hands – and damned good riddance.'

Beeman stood up reaching for his keyring. 'On your feet.'

Pierson looked malevolently at the federal officer but said nothing, not even after Gil had locked the door of his cell and stood a moment gazing in at him, before wagging his head and returning to the office.

He tossed the keyring aside, sat down and was reaching for the whiskey bottle when Douglas

Hall crossed to the chair near the door, sat down, shoved out long legs and said, 'He's a federal prisoner, Marshal. I'm a federal officer, sent out to run down the pair of them. Their crime was an attempt on the life of a federal official.'

Beeman straightened back holding the bottle. Before speaking he took one more pull from the bottle and held it out. Hall also took one more drink before passing the bottle back and watching Gil put it back in a drawer before they faced each other again.

Gil straightened up, leaned back gazing at Hall, and spoke. 'The main trouble I got with that, Mister Hall, is that his crimes were committed in my township an' if I hadn't rode my butt off, lost a lot of sleep and missed some meals — and bailed you out when he would have killed you too — there wouldn't be a prisoner.'

Douglas Hall demonstrated a characteristic which made him a successful manhunter: Stubbornness. 'Maybe there wouldn't be, but there is, and the first charges against him are federal charges. They take precedence over local charges.'

That annoyed Gil Beeman. 'Not out here they don't,' he said, and because of the unyielding expression on Hall's face, he added a little more. 'You got a warrant?'

Hall nodded. 'Two of them. One for Pierson and one for his brother.'

Gil smiled. 'Good. Now then, maybe you don't know it, but most likely you do: To extradite a prisoner for trial outside the bailiwick where he's bein' held for violation of local laws, you got to get our governor to sign an agreement for extradition.'

Hall smiled back and arose. 'I'll take care of it,' he said, nodded from the doorway and left the jailhouse on his way across to the cafe.

Beeman watched him go. His real reason for not letting the federal marshal take Pierson away with him, was about equal parts resentment – he was a confirmed States Righter – and the fact that Hall had given him about as much trouble as the assassin-brothers had.

He went out back to the bath-house behind the tonsorial parlour, took a bath and re-dressed slowly, thoughtfully. He was tired, hungry, and irritable. Maybe he was making an issue out of peevishness. After a night's sleep he'd think about it some more.

Up at Harry Lipton's saloon he encountered Doctor Wood, who told him Dorothy's men had hauled away the dead bushwhacker, which Gil already knew. He also told him that when the stage from down south had pulled into town its three passengers had jumped onto the outwardbound stage going north and despite some questions thrown at them in the corralyard, said nothing.

But Emory Wood, probably like everyone else in town, had heard vague tales and some imaginative gossip. He knew for a fact something had happened. What he wanted to know now was exactly what was behind the death of the man he had autopsied, and if, as he had heard, Gil had returned to town with another dark man.

Beeman had two straight jolts on an empty stomach. They buttressed the whiskey he and Marshal Hall had consumed at the jailhouse. He smiled at the medical man, winked and walked out of the saloon without saying a word.

Stan Hamelin, who had not returned to his barn since supper, edged up and asked the doctor what Marshal Beeman had said. He got a sour look and a mild curse. 'Nothing. Not a blessed word.'

The liveryman leaned close. 'Him an' that feller they say he locked into one of his cells, hired my wagon with the green sides, had me load it so's it'd look like a peddler's outfit, and drove south. Doc, I didn't come down in the last rain. They was settin' up a ruse sure as I'm standin' here.'

Emory Wood considered the paunchy man with the leer and the sweaty face. 'What did they say when they came back?' he asked, and the liveryman blinked a couple of times, turned as he straightened his shoulders, set his sights on the roadway and walked away. Wood and Harry Lipton watched. Hamelin did an exemplary imitation of a drunk whose effort at not appearing to be drunk allowed him to cross the room without weaving. When he reached the door he hitched up his shoulders again, pushed out into the night, and turned down in the direction of his barn.

Lipton swabbed the bartop, looked impassively at Doctor Wood and said, 'Looks like rain out there, don't it?'

Wood frowned. 'Yeah. Beautiful night. It might indeed rain. Harry, you got any idea of what's going on with Gil Beeman these days?'

The saloonman answered as he always answered such questions. 'Sure. There's fifteen stories goin' around. Every time I re-fill someone's glass they tell me another one. Which one do you want to hear?'

Doctor Wood counted out some coins, put them atop the bar and walked back out into the night where the air was utterly still, the road was empty, and diagonally opposite someone had lighted the lamps on the gateposts of the corralyard.

He was crossing Main Street when a great glow of white lightning brightened the distant mountains. It came and went in seconds. Doc Wood reached the far plankwalk slowly counting to himself. Whatever number he reached by the time the thunder arrived meant the heart of the storm was that many miles away.

There was no thunder.

He walked northward, saw lights in the stage company's office and wondered mildly about that because Dorothy closed down after the last coach left her yard. Maybe another stage was due. If it was, Doctor Wood speculated that it might be a rig hired privately to transport light freight. Or maybe it was someone in a hurry and with enough money to make the best kind of connection between where he had been and where he wanted to be.

Doc looked into the corralyard as he passed along. There were two tall logs with cotton ropes and two pulleys attached to each post for raising and lowering lighted lanterns. During the darkest days of winter the light helped yardmen see what they were doing when a stagecoach arrived after sundown. Otherwise they were only used later in the year when daylight lingered longer, if a late-coach was expected.

Neither pole had a lighted lamp atop it.

Doc's curiosity about those yard lights being lighted, told him that the light in Dorothy's office had nothing to do with a late-night coach. His curiosity dwindled down to a nubbin when he told himself that if Dorothy was actually in her office, she was probably doing what most other self-employed people around town had to do occasionally: Bring her books and accounts current.

He passed the lighted window without even looking in, his thoughts reverting again to the mystery, or whatever it was, that Gil Beeman was into up to his hocks.

At the opposite end of town Stan Hamelin listened to his nightman breathing through his mouth, exhaling fumes that would have brightly burned if someone had held a match to them.

When he had heard it all he went down to look at the stalled horses and recognised the one that had disappeared and re-appeared as well as the team animals. None of them showed signs of having been ridden hard, as in a violent manhunt.

He ignored his nightman, marched up the centre of the runway back to Main Street and struck out for home and bed. If he'd had a lick of sense he would have listened to his mother and finished normal school so's he could have become a teacher.

Teachers never had to dung out barns, doctor horses, cut corners to survive nor drink too much.

Eleven

A Dark Night

The reason for the light in the stage company's office was because Dorothy Freeman, who had been working on the books, had seen Gil Beeman striding past on his way up to the hotel, and had intercepted him.

He was now sitting with his back to the roadside wall with a cup of freshly made hot coffee awaiting her reaction to what he had told her, which was the entire story from the moment he and the federal officer had left town in Hamelin's wagon to the time they returned with Amos Pierson. His reason for being completely candid was to encourage her to be the same when he said, 'Did you see those three men who reached town on one of your stages late this afternoon?'

She nodded. 'Yes. They were polite and that was all. I think the older man would have spoken. He had gallant manners. But the other two men stood beside him like watchdogs. If he was General Joe

117

Wheeler he certainly didn't look like pictures I've seen of famous soldiers.'

Gil tasted the coffee again before speaking. He wanted to know if the general or his companions had any inkling there was to have been another attempt to kill him, but after what she had just said he decided it was pointless to ask. Instead, he said, 'The federal marshal wants to take Pierson back east with him.'

She studied his expression from her desk. 'You don't want him to do that?'

'It's not exactly that I don't want him to, Dorothy, it's that Pierson made three attempts to murder people here in our territory. This is where he should be tried and sentenced.'

She offered to re-fill his cup. He declined, drained the cup and put it aside as she made a statement that surprised him.

'You're an opinionated, stubborn man, Gil.'

He sat gazing across at her for a long moment then got to his feet. 'Thanks for the java. Goodnight.'

She sat a long time after he departed looking at the closed door, then went back to her books, but only for a short time. When she locked up for the night she stood a moment breathing storm-heavy night air and looking at the troubled sky, then went home. *For every woman there is a man. If God is willing, there are two men.* She thought about Gil Beeman until she fell asleep an hour or so later. She had never denied to herself that she was attracted to him.

But sometimes he was as immovable as stone!

Titusville was one of those frontier towns where people worked hard and slept the same way. Saturday nights were different. Rangemen arrived after a week of bruising labour to let off steam. Almost anything could happen on a Saturday night and quite often did, but during the week with rangemen in their bunkhouses and townsmen dead to the world, excepting for nights when town dogs got into a frenzy over prowling varmints in the back-alleys and around henhouses, something people could usually sleep through, Titusville was as quiet as a tomb.

For that reason when the gunfire erupted well past midnight it sounded like a cannonade. People jerked straight up in their beds with pounding hearts.

It was said later there had been five shots. There had actually been three.

Gil Beeman, sleeping the earned rest of an exhausted man, roused more slowly than other people around town, but when it finally dawned on him what the noise had been, he rolled to the edge of his bed reaching for his britches. He was stamping into his boots when the hotel proprietor came banging on his door yelling.

'Marshal! Wake Up! Someone's shootin' up the town!'

Beeman shoved his shirt-tail in with one hand and reached for his shellbelt and holster with the other hand. The hotelman continued his yelling until Beeman opened the door and glared at him.

'Go on back to bed,' he growled, and shouldered past heading for the roadway.

A few lamps had been lighted here and there but the full length of Main Street only the carriage lamp still glowed at the corralyard and at the lower end of town in front of the livery barn.

With a bad premonition he strode toward the jailhouse. When he got down there the lock was still in place, which was reassuring, but the moment he entered his office and fumbled to get the lamp going, he saw the open cell-room door, the open store-room door, and he did not have to go all the way through to see that the alley door was also hanging open.

He returned to the cell room. His prisoner was gone. That door was ajar too.

Beeman stood completely still for a long wasted moment, felt the doorlock with exploring fingers, could find no sign of violence being responsible for the door being open, and went back up to the office, took down a Winchester, his coat with the loads in its pockets from earlier, blew out the lamp and went hurrying toward Hamelin's barn.

There were scurrying old scarecrows down there, muttering, gesticulating, calling back and forth to one another until the marshal arrived, then three of them converged on him, pulling at his sleeve. He shook them off, selected one rawboned tall old gummer and said, 'What is it?'

The old man did not reply, probably because he was not entirely distinguishable when he spoke and knew it. He jerked his head and led the way down where a smoking coal-oil lamp hung suspended from a wire in the low rafters.

The light was weak but what it shone against was unmistakably a dead man. He had fallen just outside Hamelin's harness room. In fact one outstretched arm was in the doorway. Beyond that hand, perhaps eighteen inches away, inside the little room was an old grey sixgun.

The toothless oldtimer nudged Beeman and crouched forward as he stiffly pointed. Hamelin's nightman had been hit twice, once low, a grazing shot without much shocking power which had torn his britches at the hip and seared the flesh. The second shot had scored a dead-centre strike through his wishbone and his heart. It was doubtful that he had survived his encounter with his killer more than a full minute, even after he took his old weapon out to investigate something in the runway.

Men came into the barn, hastily dressed but armed. Even Harry Lipton was among them, as was the proprietor of the general store who lived a fair distance from the centre of town on the east side. He not only had a beltgun he was also carrying a double-barrelled shotgun.

Fred Barton the gunsmith had loped all the way from the upper end of town. He hadn't waited to buckle his shellbelt into place, he'd shoved a loaded Colt into his waistband, grabbed a frail-looking European hunting rifle with a big bore and two triggers. He leaned on the rifle looking at the dead man as Stan Hamelin arrived

breathless, indifferently dressed, and with pro-
fusely watering eyes. He probably also had a
headache but at the sight of his dead nighthawk
he cried out and dashed water from his eyes,
acting as though he hadn't taken on a load last
night.

He went over and dropped to one knee staring
at the corpse. Beeman pushed past, picked up the
old sixgun, spun the cylinder, stopped when he
came across the empty casing, put the old gun
gently on a rickety desk and went back out into
the runway shouldering past shocked onlookers,
most of whom were stunned into silence, but some
of whom were muttering among themselves.

Those old men were flitting around like
wraiths. Beeman ignored everyone as he went
after a horse. He was leading up a big, rawboned
bay when someone spoke among the onlookers.

'How did he do it?'

Beeman looked around at Douglas Hall. 'I'll let
you know when I catch him,' he said, and had to
shoulder more men aside to reach his saddle,
bridle and blanket. He kept his back to them all as
he worked. About the time he was buckling the
saddle boot into place on the right side, Marshal
Hall strode past carrying a shank.

Beeman ignored him. He ignored them all. He
did not do as any lifelong horseman would have
done, lead his horse out of a building before
mounting it. He swung up, kneed the big bay and
evened up his reins as he reached the back-alley.

He leaned far down. The alley had horsetracks

by the dozen, mostly overlapping other tracks. Just one set of shoe marks was not overlapping as he kneed the bay northward and continued to ride leaning far over until he was satisfied that the tracks he was watching had been made not only very recently, but also were the last tracks made last night – or this morning – by a ridden animal.

He straightened up, buttoned his coat with his right hand as he kept the animal moving and heard Titusville coming to life around him.

He couldn't hope to track Pierson very far beyond town in darkness, but he *could* continue to ride in the same direction and hope that by the time visibility returned he would have taken up enough slack to be close.

Once he reached the grassland he had to guess whether his escaped prisoner had gone northwest or northeast. Instinct told him that whether Pierson knew the easterly country or not, his last passage up yonder into the foothills and beyond had been westward. It was up there, somewhere, he had lamed that horse he'd used to flee with when he abandoned his dead brother.

It was not the kind of deduction a man would normally risk his life on, but he stood what he thought was a slightly better than fifty-fifty chance of being right.

But right or wrong he was going to ride Pierson down if it was the last thing he ever did. Three attempted murders and one outright killing was enough. More than enough.

There was a chill in the night and no stars.

Those monstrous old soiled clouds blocked out all light from above. As he rode he speculated about the rain to come. If it arrived before he could pick up good tracks again, his chance of locating Amos Pierson would dwindle drastically.

The rawboned bay horse, like many horses with his build and half-cranky disposition, was as tough as a boiled owl. When they reached the foothills the horse was just beginning to catch his second wind. He never slackened nor hung in the bit. Beeman reached down and patted his neck. To show how little he valued demonstrations of friendly encouragement, the bay flattened his ears and swung his head around in an effort to bite the marshal's stirruped foot.

Beeman yanked his head straight and snarled. The bay horse lined out arrow-straight. Evidently he'd run into riders before who knew about treacherous little tricks.

The bay shared with other rawhide-tough, half-mean dispositioned saddle animals, no fondness for riders but a great respect for those that could not be bluffed, that were just as likely to whale hell out of him as he was to bite, kick, or snake out from under them.

Normally, Gil Beeman babied his saddle animals. Tonight – this morning – he was not in that kind of a mood at all, so the bay horse decided the man on his back was no one to try his tricks on. With that settled, at least for the time being, they covered a lot of ground, got clear of the foothills and were entering the darkness of the forest when the horse detected sound Beeman did not hear, changed lead in mid-stride, which threw his rider against the saddle-forks, and tried to twist for a rearward look.

Beeman let him have enough rein to do that. When the horse was satisfied there was, indeed, another horse coming up their back trail, he settled forward again. But Beeman didn't. He rode with one hand on the cantle looking back too. It was darker than it had been. He still did not hear anything, but he nevertheless slackened pace, found a place among the trees where he could conceal himself and the bay, stepped off, placed one hand over the bay's nostrils and waited.

It was not as long a wait as it could have been. Even so, with forest darkness all around the rider was no more than a hundred and fifty feet southward before Beeman saw him.

He loosened the three bottom buttons of his coat, swept it back and palmed the holstered Colt. He had an idea who the black silhouette belonged to so he did not cock nor raise the weapon, and when the horseman was close enough, he stepped from behind a tree and said, 'What the hell do you think you're doing?'

Douglas Hall answered in the same curt manner. 'Shagging you. I already told you once, two men can handle a bushwhacker a lot better than one can. How do you know he came through here? Can you see in the dark?'

Beeman leathered the weapon, looked at the

federal officer, at his horse, which was a seal-brown but looked black in the darkness, and shook his head. 'All I know is that he don't have much more than a half-hour lead, and that he went north. The rest of it is guesswork. How about you; can you see in the dark?'

Hall's teeth shone whitely. 'No. All I know right now is that once before you walked right down someone's gunbarrel and into his sights and you're lucky he didn't kill you that time. Like that free-grazer said, Mister Beeman, I know Gawd's job is to look after fools, babies and cowboys, but that's not all He's got to do, so I came after you to help Him out.' As the federal officer stopped speaking he straightened in the saddle. 'You smell anything?'

Gil was turning back towards the bay horse when he replied. 'No. Just you.'

Hall's response was short. 'Neither do I. But these horses will. They can scent another horse, especially if he's sweating, for a hell of a distance, and that's the best we can count on until daybreak. You goin' to stand there glaring at me or get on that damned animal?'

Beeman cheeked the rawboned bay and swung up. The bay had just learned something else about his rider: Beeman was no novice.

Hall took the lead. The best either one of them could do was concentrate on not riding into a big tree or getting swept off by low limbs. Hall looked back just once. 'You afraid of the dark, Mister Beeman?'

'No, I'm not afraid of the dark!'

'You might think about it. Pierson kills from ambush. An' his horse can smell other horses too.'

Hall did not ride fast, not entirely because riding hard in mountainous country was the best of all ways to end up on foot, but also because what he had said to Gill Beeman was uppermost in his mind.

If Pierson couldn't hear them coming, because of layers of spongy pine and fir needles underfoot, he had to know sure as hell riders were looking for him, and he was a skilled bushwhacker with a long, dark night ahead of him.

Twelve
Moments Of Terror

They appeared as a pair of dark ghosts whose horses made no noise and whose silhouettes were constantly weaving back and forth among the forest giants. Beeman wondered at his companion's steady northward course. Once in the big timber, Amos Pierson could go in any direction. In fact the chances of his staying to a true-north bearing were slight, at least in Beeman's opinion, because in a forest at any time, but particularly on a moonless night, the easiest thing on earth to do was to become disoriented. Even for rangemen who developed a sixth sense about compass points early in life.

But Douglas Hall rarely deviated from his course. They struck a wide game trail and Beeman moved onto it for a fair distance before dismounting and walking ahead of his led-horse for a hundred or so yards before stopping to peer ahead.

There was nothing up there but exactly what they had been passing through for a long time; darkness, silence, forest-scents and huge old over-ripe trees.

Hall went back where Gil Beeman was dourly sitting and gestured. 'You got any idea where we're going; you know this country at all?'

The town marshal shook his head. 'Not this far north. Thirty or so miles north there's a town. That's about all I know.'

Hall nodded indifferently as he turned to gaze up ahead when he said, 'He came this way. At least someone did within the last hour or so and I got to believe it was Pierson. Who else would be riding up through here at maybe two in the morning?' Hall pointed. 'Fresh shod-horse marks, Mister Beeman. He's up there, but it'd sure help if we knew what else is up there.'

Hall returned to his mount, swung up and led out again, but from this point on he was extremely careful. He also stopped frequently, and finally he stopped altogether and swung to the ground. When Gil Beeman edged close and leaned to speak, Hall stopped him with an upraised hand. All Gil had been about to say was that the bay horse he was straddling had been walking with his head up and his ears forward for the last couple of hundred yards.

Marshal Hall motioned for Beeman to get down. They had no difficulty finding low limbs to tie their horses to. Hall had a carbine but no scabbard for it. He'd secured it to the saddle by the ring provided for that purpose.

When Beeman was ready to continue on foot the federal officer stepped close and said, 'Horse-scent.'

Beeman already knew that. He was straining to see up ahead. Visibility was very limited. Pierson could have been anywhere among the nearest trees. Beeman nudged his companion and mentioned something that amounted to a very slight favour for lawmen up in here.

'He can't see any better than we can.'

Hall's response dissolved that small advantage. 'But all he's got to do is sit there and wait. We got to keep moving until we find him. In this situation it's movement that can get people killed and Mister Pierson won't be making any, we will.'

Beeman looked at his companion. Faces were distinguishable but at no distance greater than twenty feet. 'You're such a reassurin' feller to be with, Mister Hall.'

White teeth shone as Marshal Hall smiled. He jerked his head and they started ahead with Gil Beeman moving farther to Hall's right, which was eastward. They paralleled the trail but moved along a fair distance from the trail on each side of it.

What would have helped would have been for Pierson's horse to nicker. But it didn't.

Beeman moved very cautiously and never without shelter close enough to be utilized if he had to jump for it.

It was a very large primitive area and if they

were doing all this furtive sneaking around while Pierson was still riding, they were sacrificing valuable time, and it was the element of time which had motivated Gil Beeman to leave town so rapidly after he saw Hamelin's dead night-hostler.

He understood and approved of the federal lawman's extreme caution, but there were times when a man could 'caution' himself right out of success and the farther Beeman went the more it seemed to him that this is what they were doing now.

For one thing, if Pierson had been lying in ambush waiting for them, they should have come into the area of his ambush by now. For another thing, as cold as it was getting, dawn was not far off and two men on foot sneaking around in a forest looking for someone on horseback might damned well be ridden down by the fugitive if he knew they were up there.

Beeman's heart suddenly seemed to be crowding into his throat. On his left, closer to the trail, there was a ripple of abrasive sound, as though a horse had rubbed against one of the close-spaced big trees.

He sank to one knee in an instant and shouldered the Winchester.

The noise stopped, then was audible again slightly more northward. If it was a horse he either wasn't tied or had a man on his back.

Without reason but with astonishing haste the horse – or whatever it was – reversed itself. This time Beeman could distinguish every sound. The animal was approaching down the trail in a lumbering gallop.

A single gunshot sounded from the north. The lumbering large animal picked up its gait. Beeman saw it at a distance of about twelve feet, which was as close as he had ever been to a large bear. The gunshot which had inspired greater haste in the big bear had come from the upper reaches of the trail but it was impossible to guess anything else about it – except that Beeman had not fired it and Marshal Hall could not have gotten that far up-country, so it had been either a stranger or Amos Pierson who had fired.

Beeman went in search of Douglas Hall and found him squatting beside a rough-barked old fir tree staring northward. He turned with no alarm nor surprise when Beeman came up, and waved vaguely with one hand. 'Northeast, I think. Either the trail veers in that direction a half-mile or so ahead, or he's not on the trail.'

Beeman squatted. 'Did you see the size of that bear?'

Hall looked around slowly. 'Yeah. Big wasn't he?'

'She. It was a big sow-bear.'

'I'll remember that if I ever come up in here bear hunting.'

'You might remember it before that, Mister Hall. It was hard to be sure in the dark with her movin' fast and all, but I think she was in the milk.'

Hall stared. 'In the milk?'

'Got a cub.' Hall continued to stare so Gil explained. 'If she's got a baby around in here, or maybe if Pierson shot her baby an' she was running frantically around to find it –.'

'She was running because the gunshot scairt hell out of her, Mister Beeman.'

Gil did not deny this possibility but he had hunted a lot of bears and clearly the federal lawman hadn't. 'Maybe she was, Mister Hall, but if she don't find her cub she'll be back. There's no animal on earth as far as I know as dangerous as a sow-bear with a cub. Especially if she can't find her baby and can catch man-scent.'

Douglas Hall was beginning to darkly scowl when the unmistakable roar of a large bear sounded west of them among the trees. Guns or no guns it was a sound that, especially in darkness, made every hair on the back of a man's neck stand straight up.

Beeman drily said, 'She can't find her cub an' she smells men.'

He was correct at least about the second part of what he had said. They could hear the big sow crashing over saplings and slapping against larger trees heading straight in their direction.

Beeman was arising when he said, 'And hell, I had a bath last night.'

Douglas Hall wasn't even listening. He was clutching his Winchester while backing towards the game trail. The sow sounded close enough to break into view at any moment.

Beeman caught up with Marshal Hall, took him

east of the road, and told him to kneel beside a tree and not move, not even to scratch. Hall obeyed and Gil took the same position a few yards distant.

The bear had a scent but she also needed movement, without that she would probably be unable to locate her prey. She was in a mindless rage. Even so, poor vision was characteristic even in broad daylight. All bears had poor eyesight; they stalked or charged when they could distinguish movement.

But this bear surprised Gil Beeman. When she broke out onto the trail, he knew she had his scent and Hall's scent in her face. She stood up to her full majestic height, close to eight feet, did her bear-like swinging of the head from side to side catching every vestige of every scent, dropped down to all fours making a roar that could be heard for miles, and started lumbering northward up the trail.

Douglas Hall stood up when the sow was no longer in sight, listening to her racket. She roared, then loudly growled and kept moving northward.

Gil got to his feet, leaned on his Winchester also following the old sow's noise, and wagged his head. 'It don't make sense,' he told Hall. 'Hell, she had our scent plain as day.'

'Maybe she was scairt.'

Beeman looked steadily at his companion. 'Did she look scairt to you?'

'I don't know anything about bears.'

'Glad you told me that, Marshal Hall. She wasn't scairt. Sows with babies aren't afraid of anything.' Beeman paused, listening, then made what turned out to be an accurate guess. 'She's on another scent. Maybe her cub, but whatever it is, I wouldn't want to be anywhere near when she gets up to it.'

As Beeman finished speaking he hooked the Winchester into the crook of one arm, jerked his head at Hall and started northward.

The federal marshal asked a question. 'What if she turns back?'

Beeman kept on walking. 'Then we might have to grow wings.'

'Shoot her?'

Beeman sighed. 'With thirty-thirties? If it comes to that, Mister Hall, don't aim for her head, aim for her heart and don't stop firing as long as you've got bullets. I've seen bears carryin' ten bullets in their carcasses charge right up over men.'

Hall held his silence only briefly. 'Then what in hell are we doing, trailing her?'

'I'm curious, Mister Hall. I've hunted bear all my life an' I've never seen one turn aside back down yonder like this old girl did.'

Hall said, 'You're not curious, you're crazy,' but he kept following Marshal Beeman.

Somewhere up ahead, but not very far, there seemed to be vestiges of pale light coming down through high treetops. Beeman scarcely noticed the increased visibility because a horse made a sound rarely heard by people, a deep, bawling roar of pure terror. Seconds later the horse raced past them on the east side of the trail, striking trees and feeling no pain from these encounters as it fled in blind terror.

Beeman said nothing and kept walking. He'd had only a glimpse of the horse but it was enough to satisfy him that it was the same animal Stan Hamelin had complained of because it appeared then disappeared from his barn, and that meant Amos Pierson was not far ahead.

Beeman halted when the bear made another rumbling roar. Hall came up beside him. Although a knifing dawn-chill was in the air, he was sweating. 'Where is the damned thing?' he muttered, and got no reply as Beeman started forward again, but moving slowly now.

The trail veered around a large, scabrous prehistoric rock of immense size. From this point on the trail went eastward until it was clear of the huge rock, then straightened out a little going northward again. Up ahead where there were no close-by huge trees was a little clearing of perhaps ten acres. Up there visibility was much better.

In the middle of the clearing there was one large rock, smaller than the first one but still large enough so that it was impossible to see over it or around it. The sow was out there shambling left and right on a scent.

Beeman put out his arm to keep Hall motionless for a moment then led off again to the fringe of big trees on the southwest edge of the clearing.

Beeman sank to one knee and leaned on his saddlegun. Hall looked at his profile. Beeman was almost smiling as he watched the old sow.

Beeman's mirthless little smile was a reflection of his thoughts. He had been right; the big bear was on a scent that had taken precedence over other scents. She had a cub and she was searching for it. Evidently she and her cub had been bedded down out there when Amos Pierson found the clearing and rode out into it.

The rest of Gil Beeman's speculations he kept to himself as he leaned and said, 'Watch her and watch that big rock.'

Hall nodded. 'Is her cub by the rock?'

'No. Pierson is.'

Hall hunkered down. The bear was moving back and forth. When she suddenly halted Beeman nudged his companion. 'You see a dark lump in front of her?'

Hall squinted. 'I think so. Looks like a rock.'

Beeman's retort was laconic. 'Dead cub. My guess is that when he routed them out of their bed they were close to the rock. The cub jumped up and lit out hell for leather. The sow couldn't see the cub in the tall grass but she could hear him and lit out to overtake him. From there on it's guesswork. The cub ran too close to Pierson and he shot it. The sow kept right on charging, all the way down to where we saw her. They can't see very well but can pick up a scent a half-mile off. She smelled us and charged in our direction until she reached the trail, then she picked up the scent of blood or maybe the scent of her cub. Anyway, she came chargin' back up here.'

Hall grabbed Beeman's arm. 'There he is. Pierson or someone anyway. Watch along the south side of the rock. He peeked out. Watch.'

Beeman saw the slow-moving man-shape appear around the side of the rock. He was looking for the bear and when he saw her he sucked back very quickly. The sow's keen ears detected what Beeman and Hall would have missed, the abrasive rub of boot-leather over gravel. She stopped trying to nuzzle her dead cub onto its feet and reared up seeking scent as she weaved from side to side.

She caught it.

Beeman said, 'She knows where he is.' He studied the big rock and also said, 'A man couldn't climb that thing if he was barefoot.'

The sow was back down on all fours beginning a pigeon-toed ungainly advance toward the rock.

Thirteen
An Ingredient
Of Nightmares

Gil Beeman knew about bear hunting. He also knew that while Pierson had picked up a sixgun during his escape, probably from the jailhouse office, unless he also had a rifle or a carbine he was now in trouble over his head.

He probably did not have a carbine. That thunderous gunshot that had startled the lawmen earlier, had been made by a sixgun. Carbines had a higher, more incisive sound.

Douglas Hall was on his feet as stiff as a ramrod watching the enraged sow-bear heading for the big rock. When Beeman stood up too the federal marshal said, 'She's going around it,' meaning the rock, and raised his carbine.

Gil leaned to push the Winchester aside. 'You can't bring her down from here. Not with that thing. Maybe not even with a rifle you couldn't.'

Pierson abruptly shot into sight on the north side of the rock. With the increased visibility it was easy to identify him. He was not carrying a Winchester and up to this point he had not drawn his sixgun.

Hall did not raise his carbine again but neither did he ground it.

About the time Pierson raced around the rock on the south side and disappeared behind it, the bear appeared around the north side. She was throwing up clods of grassy soil as she dug in. Her massive body was leaning toward the rock. She was growling and slobbering at the same time. To Douglas Hall who had never seen a bear run before, she seemed to cover ground about as fast as a horse could. His lips were parted, but not to say anything.

Gil Beeman shook his head without speaking. There wasn't a two-legged creature on earth who could out-run an enraged sow bear. If Pierson had any chance at all, it was to kill the bear with a shot directly into the heart. But he knew that even then she probably would not go down for several minutes, which would be long enough for her to overtake Pierson.

Hall whipped out a sentence. 'She's going to catch him!'

Beeman did not respond as Pierson shot into sight again coming around the north side of the rock. He was running in blind panic. Beeman started to yell, 'Shoot. Damn it shoot!' His shout was drowned out by the sow's deep-down snarling roar.

Pierson disappeared again around behind the rock with the sow less than fifteen feet from him. There was another of those belly-deep, snarling roars. It was followed by three rapid gunshots, another roar and no more gunfire.

Marshal Hall could not remain where he was. Whatever Amos Pierson was, he did not deserve to die this way. But Gil caught his arm and whirled him around. 'Stay out of it,' Beeman said.

Hall wrenched free and stared. 'She'll kill him!'

Gil's reply sounded loud in the hushed silence which had settled after the last roar. 'She already has. If she's wounded and you go around there ... You saw how fast she can run.' They stared at one another until Douglas Hall slumped, grounded his Winchester and, using a soiled sleeve, squeezed sweat off his face.

Marshal Hall was very shaken. He looked back at the rock, looked away then back again. Neither the sow nor Amos Pierson appeared on the north side again. It was very quiet. That sow's last roar had put everything within hearing distance to sudden terrified flight.

Even the birds were no longer among the high treetops. But the sunlight was finally out in the meadow, morning chill was dissipating, normally timid deer would have been edging out into the clearing, but there was no sign of any movement from large or small animals.

When Gil thought sufficient time had passed he said, 'Let's go,' and started walking. When they reached the cub he toed it over and saw the wide puddle of blood which had been beneath it.

Gil said, 'The damned fool. I guess he didn't know much about bears either.'

They approached the rock from the front. Beeman never took unnecessary chances and certainly not with wounded bears. They stood listening, heard nothing and started around.

The big sow was lying flat out atop Amos Pierson. The bushwhacker had been turned into raw meat by the bear's claws and rage-enhanced strength. He would not have been recognisable except for his very dark colouring and his clothing.

Hall started past and Gil grabbed him again, forced him back and raised his carbine to use as a pointer. 'Watch her nose,' he told the federal officer. 'She's not dead.'

Nor was she, although with blood running from her mouth in a scarlet stream she would die shortly. She was breathing in fluttery sighs. Each time she exhaled blood poured.

Beeman squatted in the warming sunlight to wait. Marshal Hall also squatted, but he had his carbine in both hands. The sow's little pig-eyes were fixed on them. They looked clearly able to focus but that was an illusion. Neither Hall nor Beeman could determine it, but fleas were leaving her cooling carcass.

She eventually gave a rattling, bubbly loud sigh and turned loose all over. Beeman, who had been studying her, pointed. 'There's blood showing on both sides. Pierson must have fired point-blank.

Most likely when she cuffed him to the ground
and was poised to tear him apart.'

Hall shook his head. 'Let's roll her off him and
get the hell down out of here.'

As he stood up so did Marshal Beeman, but he
did not approach the bear. He said, 'Not without
horses. That old devil weighs close on a ton and
right now she's lumpy dead weight. I'll fetch up
the horses.'

As he turned to depart Douglas Hall moved to
the north side of the rock, sat down with his back
to cold stone and leaned the Winchester aside. He
made no attempt to look back.

It was a long hike back to the place where
they'd left their horses so Marshal Beeman did
not get back to the little glade until the sun was
directly overhead, and by then even the shaded,
gloomy areas of the forest were warming up. They
would never reach the temperature of open
country, though.

They ran into an anticipated problem at once.
Their horses would not approach within a
hundred feet of the dead bear until they had
larruped them into advancing one step each time
they were hit. Even then they had to combine both
the lass ropes on their saddles and have sufficient
rope to make a couple of half hitches around the
bear's front paws.

The horses did much better when each man
held his dallies and made them pull in unison.
The horses were delighted to be moving away
from the bear. They dragged it ten yards from the

base of the rock before both riders eased up, allowed slack, got their ropes off the bear, re-coiled and lashed back into place.

The horses would go far out and around the dead bear, but would have allowed themselves to be killed before they would approach the mangled corpse of Amos Pierson. In that place there were two terrifying odours. One from the bear, the other one from blood.

Hall and Beeman had to carry the corpse down into the middle of the little clearing before the horses would even tolerate it. Beeman swore. There was nothing to wrap Pierson in, and hauling him back to Titusville behind a cantle would get blood on saddle skirts, and blood absorbed by saddle leather could not be removed. It would also stain a horse.

Stan Hamelin would be mad as a hornet, but they tied the body behind Beeman's cantle anyway. Neither of them said a word until they came upon a little brawling snow-water creek and swung off to tank up their animals and use gritty mud to wash blood off their hands and arms. Marshal Hall made a comment. 'If I live to be a hundred I don't expect to see anything like that again.'

Beeman was too busy washing to respond, but as they were riding away from the creek he said, 'Some folks might call it retribution. Maybe; but it seems to me it never would have happened if Pierson had used his head. Hell, a man don't have to be savvy about bears. Even an old mammy-cow will charge you when she's got a baby calf.'

Hall did not dispute this, he simply said, 'But she can't tear a man to pieces.'

By the time they reached the foothills afternoon was well advanced. They had to stop to re-tie the corpse and something that may have been building up for a long time happened. The rawboned bay horse decided he did not want that soggy carcass on his back. He waited until Beeman was toeing in to mount, jerked enough rein through Gil's finger to get his head down, and the moment Beeman reached the saddle the bay horse took to him like a cougar.

He could buck. He could sunfish and hit the ground stiff-legged with a thousand pounds of jolt under his saddle, and despite Gil's best effort to get his head up, the bay horse kept it down between his knees.

Douglas Hall got close, nearly rubbed Beeman out of the saddle and roughly caught the reins, dallied one of them and set the bay horse back on his haunches. He was sweating, orry-eyed and sucking air like a bellows when Gil dismounted, checked his rigging, checked the plight of the corpse, then got set squarely down and kicked the bay horse in the rear as hard as he could kick.

The horse gave a tremendous jump and was wrenched harshly around by Hall's dally. Gil walked up behind him and repeated the punishment, took back the reins, did not say a word, toed in and swung up, evened up his reins, held them tightly and kneed the bay horse out.

For a full mile the horse walked along without looking left or right, with his little ears pinned straight back. He had just learned the last thing he had to learn about the man who was riding him. He did not have to like him. He did not have to always obey rein-pressure instantly, but he had better never again forget to respect him.

They had Titusville's rooftops in sight about sundown, but did not reach the place until dusk, which never lasted long anyway, had darkened into evening with full darkness to follow shortly.

By the time they were passing southward in the direction of the livery barn, using the west-alleyway, the town's meagre week-day nightlife was coming to life over at Lipton's saloon, and that was about all the noise they heard until they swung off out back of Doctor Wood's place, carried their gory burden into his little shed, got back astride and went all the way down to the livery barn where they dismounted for the last time and led their animals up the runway.

It was unusual for the liveryman to be down there after supper, but he was not only in the barn, he was standing in the middle of the runway talking to an old man, and stopped talking to stand with his mouth agape as he watched Beeman and his companion bring up the horses.

They both nodded at Hamelin, without a word looped their reins, nodded again and strode towards the front roadway leaving the two men back in the runway staring after them.

Mid-way in the direction of the cafe Hall said,

'Good thing it was dark back there.'

Beeman was holding the cafe door and standing aside when he replied. 'Yeah, but by morning he'll see the blood an' come up to the jailhouse bellowing like a gored bull.'

They had the cafe to themselves, which was a relief. Their appearance told the world they had been through a difficult time. It also told the world those specks of dried dark maroon were blood. The rest of it the world, and the big-eyed cafeman, could surmise because Hall had his marshal's badge pinned to his shirt. Both the cafeman's customers had been somewhere over the past twenty-four hours where there had been serious violence.

When they arose to pay the cafeman said, 'You want some stew'n coffee for your prisoner, Mister Beeman?'

Gil shook his head, led the way out into the settling night and halted upon the opposite plankwalk as he said, 'He's yours, Mister Hall.'

The federal officer's brows slowly drew inward. 'What are you talking about?'

'He is yours. You wanted to haul him back east to be tried. Well, go right ahead.'

'That's not much of a joke, Mister Beeman.'

Gil smiled, nodded and stepped past as he said, 'Best I can do tonight.'

Up at the roominghouse the proprietor watched him enter, exchanged nods as Beeman went past, then said, 'What you been doin', butcherin' sheep?'

Beeman unlocked his door then stood looking back when he replied. 'No. Hotelman,' walked in, kicked the door closed and let go a big sigh as he shed his hat, shellbelt, coat and went to stand by the roadside window looking sombrely southward down Main Street.

Somewhere up north, perhaps between Titusville and Denver, there was a little elderly soul with a scraggly white beard, precious little hair on his scalp who wore baggy britches stuffed into military boots, who was on his way back east thinking he had survived a stage holdup, or maybe he suspected it had been an attempt to kill him, but whatever he thought he did not have any idea that by just passing through a place he probably did not even recall as named Titusville, he had intervened in the lives of a dozen people, had been instrumental in two deaths, and had left a legacy people would not forget.

Beeman was yanked out of his reverie by a canine chorus somewhere across from the hotel, most likely in the alley over there, where some foraging varmint had upset a metal barrel. Probably a racoon. They had been getting very bold lately.

He shucked out of his clothing, hung most of it on the floor and crawled between flannel sheets, and for no logical reason at all thought back to something he'd been told before riding out: 'You are an opinionated and stubborn man ....'

He hitched up onto his side, groaned and closed his eyes. The Good Lord had a sense of irony. He had to have to create handsome women, then insert a shred of rankling into their dispositions.

Fourteen

The Storm

Beeman was making coffee on the jailhouse stove, feeling reasonably human again, half-full of pancakes lying like lead in his stomach and no longer tired, when his first visitor of the morning arrived.

It was Doctor Wood. He wasn't angry but neither was he jovial as he sat down, wrinkled his nose at the smell of boiling coffee, and said, 'What happened to him?'

Gil drew off two cups, handed Emory Wood one and returned to the desk with the other cup. 'First, he tried to out-run a bear. Then he didn't start shootin' until she was breathin' in his face.'

'Did he kill her?'

'Yes. An' she fell on top of him.'

Doctor Wood considered the coffee. 'Well, what am I supposed to do with him?'

'Maybe wrap him in something so's he can be buried beside the other one, who was his brother.'

Wood continued to look into his cup. 'When was the last time you changed the grounds in that coffee pot?'

'Last week. Why?'

'Because if you'll bottle this stuff I'll buy it from you to use as embalming fluid.'

Beeman tasted the coffee. It seemed all right to him. 'You're too finicky, Emory.'

The medical practitioner did not deny this. He even tasted the coffee. Then he put the cup aside and rummaged in a coat pocket until he found what he was seeking, and tossed it atop Marshal Beeman's desk.

It was a key. Not as thick as most brass keys but equally as long. Beeman stared at it. 'Where did you find it?'

'In a little buckskin pocket sewed inside his right boot.'

The marshal arose, took down his keyring, held the key against the key he used on the cell doors, leaned so that Wood could see how perfectly they matched, then sat back down gazing at the key. 'That son of a bitch was a real professional, Emory. All right; from now on before anyone gets locked into my cells he's goin' to strip to the hide and leave everything but his pants and shirt in my office.'

Doctor Wood eyed the coffee but did not reach for it. 'I met Dorothy this morning on my way down here. She'd heard you and another man got back to town last night covered with blood.' The doctor's gaze went to Beeman's face and remained there. 'She was worried sick.'

'What about?'

Doctor Wood arose, straightened his coat and looked a little disgustedly at Marshal Beeman. 'If you don't know, it's not my business to tell you. I'll have that feller wrapped and sent down to be measured for a box in a couple of hours.'

Beeman had finished his coffee and was sinking the cup in a bucket of greasy water behind the stove when his second visitor walked in. He was looking over his shoulder as he did so, and looked forward only when Marshal Beeman said, 'Good morning, Mister Hall.'

The federal officer nodded, took the same chair Emory Wood had used and said, 'Those storm clouds are almost directly over Titusville. But the sun's shining through in a couple of places.'

Beeman filled two more cups and took another one to the desk with him. 'It'll rain,' he stated. 'I can feel it in my bones. The stockmen will like it and so will I, because it'll make the countryside too muddy for them to ride in to tree the town come Saturday night.'

Having dispensed with this traditional method of beginning range country conversations, Beeman eyed the other tall, muscular man. 'Doc's goin' to wrap him in sacking or something so's you can haul him away with you.'

Hall drank half the coffee. He gazed at Beeman over the cup's rim. 'When are you going to let up about me insisting on extraditing him?'

'When you leave town. How d'you like that coffee?'

Hall looked from Beeman to the cup and back. 'Fine. Is something wrong with it?'

'I don't think so, but there was a feller in here a while back who called it embalming fluid.'

Hall drained the cup and smacked his lips. 'Well, maybe next time if you used a little less chewing tobacco … I paid for a ride north on the first stage heading that way this afternoon. Thought I'd come by and say, "thanks".'

'For what?'

Hall considered the empty cup. 'For teaching me something about bears. Not for anything else because I'd have run him down if you hadn't been in the way.'

Beeman was trying to find an appropriate reply when Marshal Hall spoke again as he was arising to put the cup aside. 'I wanted a few words with that good-looking woman who owns the local stages this morning. I wanted to know all I could find out about her three passengers. She didn't know anything except that they switched stages and kept heading north.'

Beeman nodded. He already knew this.

Hall went to stand in the doorway before speaking again as he looked back. 'She wanted every blessed detail of what happened up yonder yesterday. I thought maybe she was one of those folks who like gory stories. That wasn't it. She was worried about you – how close you came to getting hurt and all.' The federal officer smiled. 'I told her you were never in any danger at all as long as I was along, because I knew what that bear would do and kept you from going out into the clearing. You know what she did? Kissed me ... Hope we meet again some day, Marshal.'

Beeman took two more empty cups to sink them in the wash-bucket behind the stove. He was considering making a round of the town when Stan Hamelin arrived. This time Beeman offered no coffee. The pot was down to its grounds and he did not feel much like pouring in more water because if the liveryman got comfortable with a cup of java, he might go on jawboning for an hour.

Hamelin was a traditionalist. He said, 'Storm's coming. Looks like it could be a real gully-washer.'

Beeman returned to his chair and sat down. He nodded.

The liveryman shoved out thick legs and considered his cracked boots. 'Do you know that blood don't come out of leather?'

Beeman nodded again, regarding the older man stonily.

'An' neither does it come out of horsehair without one hell of a lot of work.'

Beeman replied vocally this time. 'Stan, a bear mauled the man an' we didn't have a damned thing to wrap him in, otherwise we wouldn't have brought him back like that.'

The liveryman made a practical statement. 'You could have left him up there. For the stories I've heard around town no one would miss him, or the other one.' Hamelin's pale grey eyes lifted to the marshal's face. 'What in the hell was that all about? You got to remember that I helped you

with that wagon and all the junk we piled into it
so's someone would think you was peddlers and
emigrants, or something besides the law.'

A dark shadow had appeared at the north end of
town and worked its way southward toward the
lower end. When it blocked out sunlight in front of
the jailhouse Beeman's office got noticeably dark,
so he went to look out the doorway.

Behind him the liveryman spoke without
moving from the chair or looking around. 'I told
you. It's goin' to rain like hell.'

When Beeman neither turned back nor left the
doorway the liveryman levered up out of the chair
and went to stand nearby looking out where the
rain-shadow was not moving. He shouldered past
to leave as he said, 'Someday, when we both got
plenty of time, maybe we can share a bottle at the
saloon an' you can tell me what the hell's been goin'
on around here.'

Beeman agreed to do that, some day, and
watched Hamelin hike more rapidly than he
usually walked in the direction of his barn. Everyone had to prepare for what was coming and
liverymen had more to cover and shelter than most
merchants.

Northward, a mud-wagon belonging to the local
stage company came into town with slack traces. It
looked like a stagecoach but there were noticeable
differences including wider tyres and more expo-
sure for passengers. It wheeled up into the corralyard. After it had passed from sight Beeman
continued to gaze up in that direction. Maybe

Dorothy would come out.

She didn't. She spoke from behind him, making him start as he turned. She looked as though she might laugh at having startled him. She had been down at the harness works to ascertain when some harness she needed would be repaired.

Gil stepped aside for her to enter the office but she remained under the warped overhang holding a light shawl around her shoulders. 'I'm glad things worked out satisfactorily for you up yonder where you and Marshal Hall found that dark man.'

He smiled at her. 'Sure was glad to have him along, Dorothy.'

'Yes, I imagine you were. In that kind of situation it's best to have a man with you who knows about bears.'

There was a twinkle in her eye that should have warned Beeman but it didn't. 'Yes, indeed it is, ma'am.'

'Except that he didn't know about bears, did he?'

Beeman finally saw the twinkle. 'Well now, what makes you think that?'

'Because he called it a "she-bear" and even I know females are called sow-bears.'

'... I could brew up a pot of coffee, Dorothy.'

'I wish I could, Gil, but with this storm coming ...'

'Sure. Another time.'

She put her head slightly on one side looking up at him. 'But if you'd have the time to come up to

the corralyard with me, when I've done everything that can be done, we could sit in the office,
listen to the rain and have some coffee.'

He had never noticed it before, but she had a
sturdy little pulse in her throat. Or maybe it just
hadn't been as noticeably strong as it was right
now. And she was looking him squarely in the eye.

He briefly hung fire, then said, 'Wait,' and
stepped inside for his coat and hat. As an
afterthought he also got his black raincoat from
the store room. When he returned she eyed the
rubber coat but said nothing until he spoke as he
had his back to her to lock the jailhouse door. 'Just
in case you throw me out before the storm passes.'

'Why would I do that?'

He turned pocketing the key. 'Because you can
be pig-headed at times, an' also because you're
used to giving orders to yardmen, an' I guess I
could put up with the pig-headedness but the first
time you give me an order I'll start walking.
That's why I'm bringing along the raincoat.'

He would have started northward but she did
not move. 'Have I ever given you an order, Gil?'

'You've come close a couple of times.'

A gust of chilly, damp air came through from
the north. She held the shawl a little closer as she
faced into the wind. As they walked, heads down
into the wind, she had to raise her voice to be
heard. 'Gil, there are men, then there are men.'

He looked around at her lowered head. 'Is that a
fact?'

'I mean, my yardmen either aren't happy

working for a woman, so I have to act like a man with them, or else they act like I'm a child and they have to indulge me. That's why I give orders. It's also why when I tell them something I don't change my mind.'

He walked leaning into the wind half the distance to her corralyard before speaking again. 'You know something, Dorothy? You're pretty as a picture. Especially with the wind blowin' against you like that.'

Her head came up in astonishment, colour rose in her face. In all the years they had known one another he had never made that kind of a remark to her before. She was a little nonplussed so all she could think to say was: 'Do you think so?'

'I've always thought so. Even when you called me names.'

'Names?'

'Opinionated and stubborn.'

'Well. You are, Gil. But I wasn't calling you names I was simply saying what I know about you. And it didn't mean I disapproved.'

They reached the corralyard gates and turned in where the wind could not reach them. Her yardmen were busy in all directions getting ready for the storm. Gil watched for a while then smiled at her. 'Go give a few orders, boss-lady.'

She smiled back but her eyes sparked at him. 'No need. Let's go inside and make that coffee. And if it rains a long time you can stay as long as you like.'

He stopped at the doorway. 'As long as I like?'

She moved past into the office without looking up at him. 'Yes. As long as you like.'

The storm struck with no more preliminary than that damp wind. It differed from other late downpours in that it did not begin with a light spattering of rowel-sized raindrops. One minute the wind was blowing, the town was dry, and the next minute marching walls of water which had drenched the mountains, the foothills and the rangeland, swept over Titusville. For a while dry earth could absorb the water, but not for long.

It also made conversation difficult inside buildings. Dorothy made a pot of coffee while Beeman checked the iron stove, put in a couple of fir scantling and re-set the damper.

He went to stand by the roadside window where visibility was distorted by waves of water striking the glass. Even so, familiar things were discernible, such as Barton's gunshop across the way with steel shutters across its windows, and farther south, down at Lipton's saloon, heavy wooden doors had been barred behind the louvred spindle doors.

There was neither a two-legged nor four-legged critter the full length of Titusville's roadway, and wouldn't be until the storm's fury abated.

Dorothy had dispensed with the shawl. She had also repaired the damage to her hair caused by the wind. When she came up beside Beeman he turned and either could not or did not make an attempt to hide his look of admiration. She smiled at him, and yelled, 'It'll be ready in a short while. I don't like weak coffee, do you?'

He didn't try to answer aloud. He shook his head and turned back to look into the roadway. If this storm lasted any length of time it would wash gullies in the roadway a man could bury a horse in.

Her fingers crept into his slack hand, startling him but he did not look around nor react with surprise. He gently exerted pressure and she just as gently squeezed back. She yelled again. 'Women shouldn't swear, should they?'

'No, I guess not. Why?'

'Because right now I'd feel silly yelling things I'd like to tell you. It's exasperating.'

He turned, smiling. 'Save 'em!' he yelled back. 'I'll save mine. Storms don't last forever. Leastways I've never heard of one that did.'

She leaned against him. He eased an arm around her. Waves of water continued to lash the town. Those ponderous rain clouds were still moving though, which meant that, as he had said, the storm wouldn't last forever.